Spy of Brunswick Town

By

Edith Edwards

Edith Edwards

Other books by Edith Edwards

The Ghosts of Bald Head Island

From Hallowed Ground

Tales Through Time: Women of the South
(short story collection co-authored with Joan Leotta)

Cover Photo:
Helena Grace Upshaw

To Larry Maisel and Henry Hall—two extraordinary men—one living and the other with the angels—men who love and appreciate all things Southern, especially the women.

To Ponder....

But they that wait upon the Lord shall renew their strength; they shall mount up with wings as eagles; they shall run and not be weary; and they shall walk and not faint. Isaiah 40:31 KJV

"With our imagination as well as our eyes, that is to say like artists, we must see not just their faces but the life behind and within their faces."
Frederick Buechner, <u>Listening to Your Life</u>

"Remember me not for the ill I've done but for the good I've dreamed."
Frederick Buechner, <u>Listening to Your Life</u>

"...there is another class of men—at their best they are poets, at their worst artful dodgers..."
Frederick Buechner, <u>Listening to Your Life</u>

Spy of Brunswick Town

By

Edith Edwards

Mariah
Chapter 1

The snake kept her frozen in place with one beady eye. It knew she was in its territory, but was not agitated enough to strike.

I can out wait you, she thought, I've out waited worse.

Absentmindedly, Mariah fingered the red triangular birthmark at the base of her neck. She stroked it when she was nervous. "The red-tailed hawk," her Grannie Long had told her. "You've got the mark of a hawk's tail—your protector. With every generation someone has the mark. You are blessed."

"Poppycock," her ma had scoffed at her mother-in-law's musings.

Eventually, the creature grew tired and slithered off through the underbrush.

Mariah stayed in place until she was sure she was safe. The swamp was full of dangers—and not only reptilian. She heard the deep croak of a bullfrog echoing across the brackish water. The smell of salt marsh and pluff mud reminded her she was near the sea.

Being a child of the swamp, she knew how to maneuver through the brambles that groped for her as she slid under hanging limbs and over sunken logs. Her small frame let her squeeze through openings in the forest that would have hindered a larger person.

*****

She was late. Lieutenant McAllister had promised to meet her at two o'clock. The slant of the sun proved that it was at least four. Trudging on, she sloughed through mud and pushed aside underbrush, slapping mosquitoes as she went.

The Brody home stood on a small rise above the marsh as if it had oozed up from the muck. The exterior walls were the color of dried mud—having been made from local material.

Mariah had been here in happier times. She remembered balls and parties—before the Yankees came.

The scream echoed through the woods, long before she reached her destination. By the time she got to the side of the house, all she heard were muffled sobs and a gruff man's voice.

"Shut up, woman. You'll bring the other soldiers. Then they, too, can have their way with you."

No answer, just more sobs.

Mariah peered through the door, frightened and

curious, but afraid to attract attention.

Bess Brody lay sprawled on the floor, the skirt of her once elegant dress spread around her. Lieutenant Thaddeus McAllister, 12th New York Cavalry, stood over her, methodically buttoning his pants.

She gasped at what she saw. McAllister turned and glared at her. "So you finally got here. Too bad. You could have been the lucky one."

As she ran to Bess, McAllister grabbed her arm. "I don't have time to wait for you to coddle that simpering fool," he growled. "Have you got the money?"

Showing him the money belt she clutched she growled at him, "Have you got information?"

He snatched the bag and strode to a table in the next room. Tossing it down, he groped at the rawhide ties. Raw greed covered his face. As he began counting the money, he grumbled. "Women, I hate dealing with the likes of you. You're late, you're weak, and you always get in the way."

Mariah left Bess and followed the lieutenant. "You mean I always deliver what I promise. Now tell me what you know."

"I'll tell you, but only because I like your gold."

He finished counting and turned to face her. Bess continued to whimper from the floor. "General Wessells is planning to leave Plymouth—to make another push against Fort Branch. He believes it's vital to reach the railroad bridge at Weldon and break your Confederate supply line between the port of Wilmington and Lee's

Army of Northern Virginia. Says it's 1864 and high time we got this war over with."

She ignored the last comment. "That's no news. Wessells has tried that continually. He can't get by our forces at Rainbow Bluffs. We've blocked his route on the Roanoke River."

"Then my guess will be that he'll go by land. I don't know. I'm not the General. I do know that we've been amassing supplies for an overland march."

"Still, you've told me nothing that we haven't been expecting. You need to give me more information."

McAllister glared. "You're a saucy wench, aren't you? I've a mind to teach you a lesson, but then you couldn't supply me with the gold you Rebs have hidden. And I do plan a comfortable retirement in Barbados. Perhaps you'd like to join me? Your womanly charms could keep me happy."

Mariah shuddered. "What else?" she demanded. "Tell me more or you'll see that our gold dries up."

"I know the date. We've been told to expect to move around April 18th. Someone in your web of spies will want to know that.

"I have to go." McAllister threw the satchel over his shoulder. "I've been gone too long as it is." With a sidelong look at Bess he chuckled. "I must say, the afternoon's entertainment has been worthwhile."

He gathered his hat and shoulder bag and stomped out of the house.

Mariah heard it then, as she had never heard it

before—the hoarse shriek of a red-tailed hawk. "Kree-eee-ar" echoed through the pines, a high pitched scream, followed by a downward slur.

Three times the hawk screeched, then was silent. Intuitively, Mariah knew the cry was for her. Her pa had many failings, but he knew nature. He had taught her birdcalls, including the hawk's. This hawk was angry and agitated. It echoed her feelings.

I hate Yankees, especially McAllister, she thought, and then went to tend Bess.

Bess sat on the floor, staring. Her face was cold and grey as if she were in shock. But she looked up and opened her hand.

"What's that, Bess? Why it's solid gold—some sort of medal."

"I stole it out of McAllister's pack while he was in the other room. Take it. Maybe you can sell it."

Mariah stared at the gold star topped with an eagle and hanging from a red, white and blue ribbon. "It's the Medal of Honor," she gasped. "It's only awarded for exemplary service. It's the highest medal awarded by the Yankees. How could someone like McAllister receive such a medal? See, his name is engraved on the back."

"Take it," Bess repeated. "I want no part of the man."

"I'll take it, but I doubt I'll sell it. This may prove to be more valuable than money."

Hands on hips, Mariah gently admonished her

friend. "Why were you here? You know you shouldn't be here when I meet with McAllister."

"I thought you'd been here and gone. You're usually not this late. I fell ill working in the field and came inside." Her voice was little more than a whisper— strained, raspy, but with a note of accusation.

After helping Bess from the floor and getting her a glass of water, Mariah left. She knew that Bess was strong. She'd lost her young husband in this dreaded war and had survived. She would survive this. Her field hands would soon come in from trying to eke a few vegetables from her meager garden. They would care for her.

Mariah left the Brody home and considered her options. It was warm for early March. Since it was almost dark, she could chance the roads. Her home was five miles to the south, but she often walked that distance.

She had important information for Lee's army that she must convey as soon as possible. The Civil War, or War of Northern Aggression as Mariah preferred to label this conflict, was going badly for the South. Mariah knew that as a spy, she had a duty to do what she could to turn the tide.

I could go to the nearest garrison and tell what I know. That would be Ft. Fisher, outside of Wilmington. But that would be a three-day ride and I have no way of knowing if I will be taken seriously. No, better to work through my established network, a team called The Group.

Pa will be angry I've been gone all afternoon, she thought. His bitterness since Ma died and he lost a leg at Gettysburg is palpable. With luck, he'll have drunk himself into a stupor and leave me alone.

Her pa was snoring by the fireplace when she got home. She knew he would sleep there all night and wake in a foul mood in the morning. She planned to be gone by then.

Too excited to eat or sleep, she gathered what rations she could find for the journey. Then she sat by the window and waited for first light.

At dawn, Mariah stole to the barn and hitched Lucy to the buckboard. As the only schoolteacher in the county, she had been allowed to keep a horse to drive to the schoolhouse. The Army had conscripted the rest of their animals.

After crossing the Lockwood Folly River, Mariah settled in for an uncomfortable ride. The land was parched from lack of rain and the vegetation showed it. Lucy clopped along, throwing clouds of dust and billowing sand every time her hooves struck the road. Mariah knew that her arms and dress would be a sight by the time she reached her destination.

After the initial excitement of leaving home, Mariah's mind turned to more sober thoughts. What will the children think when they arrive at school this morning and I'm not there? They're good children and the school offers them diversion from their dreary, poverty-stricken lives.

And Pa. He would get by, but he would worry. As harsh a man as he's become, I know he loves me. I remember happy times when we would walk through the swamp and call out the names of plants, animals, and birds. Thanks to him, I am able to navigate the marshes as easily as any swamp creature.

Mariah realized that another gift her father had given her was the faith she used to have. Every Sunday he would insist that the family hitch up their wagon and go to the small church in Shallotte. They would stay all day—attending the service, visiting with neighbors, and eating from their picnic basket.

The times she treasured most were the nights her pa drew her onto his lap and read Bible stories. His deep voice brought alive the travels of Abraham, the trials of the children of Israel, the birth of Jesus. Her pa had been a religious man, but it had been many years since he'd pulled his well-worn Bible from the shelf.

She had given up on religion, too. "What kind of loving God would let his children suffer the way I've seen friends and neighbors suffer these last few years?" she often whispered to herself.

"Mr. and Mrs. Markey down the road had to watch as their son Ned was brought home—his lifeless body strapped across a horse led by his brother. My students have little food and are shabbily clothed. Maybe God is smiling on the Yankees, but He's forgotten the South."

Her pa guessed that her work was dangerous. She'd never told him what she did when she was gone on her long absences, but he presumed it was for the war effort. Too often she had voiced how the Yankees had disrupted her life. Just when she had planned to further her education, the war came and she was forced to stay at home.

For her pa, the war was over. He was lost in the morass of alcohol and bitterness. Living with him had become unbearable for Mariah. He was not the man he used to be.

Perhaps none of us are the people we were before the war, Mariah thought. She remembered McAllister and the medal in her pocket. What was he like before the war? Now he's motivated by greed, but maybe he wasn't always like that.

Mariah was frustrated. "I wish we could leave the buckboard and I could ride you bareback," she told her horse. "But that would attract attention. Better that travelers think I'm on my way to school."

By noon they had reached Wilmington; by nightfall they were in Warsaw. The Wilton boys weren't surprised to see her. They were used to her showing up at odd times in her work as a spy. The pitchfork was jabbed into the ground by their gatepost—a sign they were trusted members of The Group.

"Mariah," Jake Wilton shouted as she turned Lucy

toward their homestead. "We thought you might come. We haven't seen you in awhile. Do you have news for us?"

Mariah showed him the embroidered pitchfork badge on her belt, and he did the same.

"This seems like a lot of trouble," he grumbled. "I've known you for years. Why do I have to wear this thing around my waist all the time? Seems sort of sissy to me."

"Jake," she laughed, "quit complaining. It's for the best. Even though we know each other, there are members of our alliance we don't know. I saw your pitchfork by the gate. It's a part of us. Ever since William said he'd like to take a pitchfork and pitch those Yankees to Canada, the pitchfork has been the emblem of The Group."

Jake nodded in agreement. "William is a smart man and a good leader. Now tell me, do you have news for us?"

"I do, Jake. Help me unhitch Lucy and I'll tell you what I know."

Over their supper of cold beans and cornbread, Mariah told the three middle-aged bachelors what she'd learned from McAllister. Soon she pushed away her bowl, the food half eaten. The men were good-hearted, but their meals lacked a woman's touch.

"So you plan to ride by yourself to our next post?" Thomas asked. "We have loyal people at every stop, but you needn't be alone. We'll go with you."

"That will take too long. It's already mid-March. I need to tell Lee what the Yankees plan."

"And you think you can just waltz into Lee's camp and he'll see you?" Ben Wilton was skeptical. "You've made a name for yourself as a spy, Mariah, but it may not be that easy. And I agree with the boys. You can't travel alone."

"Then one of you goes with me. We can take horses and leave the buckboard. Jake, you're the youngest. We'll ride together and tell everyone you're my husband."

The staunch bachelor blushed deep crimson. "B-b-but, Mariah, we might have to, well you know, have to…"

"Yes, we might have to sleep together. I'll give you a break tonight, husband, dear. Let's get some rest so we can leave early in the morning."

It took them five days to get to Northern Virginia where Lee's army was bivouacked. They had set a steady pace. At night they were welcomed by members of the Group and given comfortable lodging. At each stop, they made certain a pitchfork was by the gatepost and that their hosts wore the badge.

"You can't be too careful," Mariah told Jake.

"You're right," Jake hung his head and whispered, "I wish we didn't have to sleep together."

Again she reminded him, "We have to be careful, Jake. The fewer people who know about our disguise, the better. And believe me, I'd rather not sleep with you—you snore."

"Humph!" was his reply.

A troubling sight on their journey was the men they passed who were heading south. Many were limping or had other injuries. All were thin and poorly clothed. Not the gallant young boys who had ridden off a few short years before, vowing they'd be home soon after they had whipped the Yankees. They averted their eyes when Mariah and Jake passed.

"Deserters," Mariah scoffed. "Leaving before the war is won."

"Ah, child. For many of these boys the war is over. They're wounded and dispirited. Many have left homes and families. They've got crops to put in if they want to keep their land. And truthfully, unless England or France steps up to help us, we've lost this war."

"Don't say that, Jake, it's bad luck! We will win this war."

Jake didn't answer but stopped to offer food and water to a man who looked more bedraggled than the rest. The man tipped his hat, and resumed his trek down the dusty road.

"Why do you feed them Jake? They're cowards. I'd never have anything to do with a deserter."

"They're our boys, Mariah. Our sons, husbands, and fathers. That man I just helped? You can be sure some woman somewhere is longing for the sight of him. Maybe that little bit of aid will be what gets him home."

"Like I said, I'd never have anything to do with a deserter."

Chapter 2

Their last hosts told them how to find General Lee. "His headquarters are on the Rappahannock near Chancellorsville. Something's getting ready to happen there. You'll have to ask for the General—his exact whereabouts are a closely guarded secret. Show them the badge. That should count for something."

At noon that day they met their first Confederate sentry. "Halt! Identify yourself!" he shouted. A young boy, perhaps sixteen years old and obviously terrified, challenged them.

"We must see Gen. Lee!" Mariah insisted. "We are members of The Group and we have news." As she spoke, she raised her shirt and showed him the pitchfork badge.

'The what? You're part of what?"

"The Group—we have information that will aid the Confederacy."

"Yeah, and my grandmother is..."

"What's all this noise," an older, surly, voice

growled. "If there are any Yankees within a hundred miles they'll know where we are."

"These people, Sergeant," the young sentry began, "they say they're part of something called..."

"Bennie!" Jake shouted, jumping off his horse and rushing to meet the older soldier. "Bennie, it's you! We heard you'd been killed at Gettysburg."

The older soldier stepped back, and then threw his arms around Jake. "Darn near was, Cousin. Darn near was. Got my leg all shot up. Now I'm not good for much of anything except standing guard duty with babies like this lad.

"But what are you doing here?" he continued. "And who is this beautiful young woman? Jake, you old fox. Did you finally go and get yourself married?"

"Please sir," Mariah interjected. "I'm not Jake's wife. We're part of a network called The Group. I guess you'd say we're spies. We have important information for Gen. Lee."

Sergeant Bennie drew back and leveled his rifle at them. "Show me your badge," he barked.

"It's me, Bennie." Jake sounded devastated that his cousin challenged him, but showed his badge.

Mariah did the same.

"Sorry, Cousin, Ma'am" he apologized. "Guess you haven't heard. Some of The Group have turned traitor. The Yankees are paying them well for their treachery. I knew you, Jake. I know you're not a traitor. But I didn't know the woman."

"Can you help us find Gen. Lee?" Mariah asked. "Our message is urgent."

"Well, you're in luck. Gen. Lee is camped five miles away. But why must you see him? There are lots of other officers who could take a message."

"I don't want to give our message to anyone except him. It's too important. There must be a way to see the General."

Sergeant Bennie smiled at Mariah's determination. "I do have an in that might help you. I have a way with horses and I nursed his Traveler through a nasty leg wound. He'll see you if I ask."

They arrived at Gen. Lee's camp at dusk. As they passed the troops, Mariah received her share of whistles and catcalls. She also received three marriage proposals. Seeing the meager rations the men were eating saddened Mariah and Jake, but they were not surprised. They were eating no better at home.

As soon as Sergeant Bennie told the guard outside of Lee's tent who he was, the General himself came out. Mariah was shocked at his appearance. She had seen him before the war at a ball in Wilmington—a handsome, dashing man. This old soldier was bent and grey.

"Ah Bennie," Gen. Lee said, coming up to shake the sergeant's hand. "Traveler sends his regards. And who—why Mariah. Mariah Long. What on earth would bring you to this god-forsaken place?"

"Gen. Lee." Mariah curtsied. For her to do less in the presence of this great man would have been beneath her sense of honor. "I'm honored you remember me."

"Remember you? You were the most beautiful woman at the ball that night—excluding my own dear Mary, of course. Here, stand up, let me look at you." Lee took her hands and kissed her on the cheek. "Ah," he whispered. "It's been so long, so long."

"Gen. Lee," Jake stepped forward and broke the spell. "I'm Jake Wilton. Mariah and I have news for you. We are members of The Group. We must speak to you in private."

"The Group." The General lowered his head as a slow, red flush creeped up his neck and onto his face. "I've received bad news about that band lately. Seems there are rotten apples in the barrel. Even though I know you, do you have identification?"

Jake and Mariah pulled out their badges and showed them to the General. He nodded his head in approval.

"I must go, Jake," Bennie said. "I've been gone from my post too long. That young fool has probably shot himself in the foot by now." He wrapped his arms around his cousin. One small tear glistened in his eye, and fell onto Jake's shoulder.

Gen. Lee showed them into his tent and called for brandy. They told him what Mariah had learned from

Thaddeus McAllister.

"April 18th, you say," Lee stroked his beard and considered what they had said. "I knew Wessells would try again. That railroad is too important. And your source says they're planning an overland attack. I will meet with my staff immediately and decide what's to be done. In the meantime, we will find you proper sleeping quarters."

"Please, sir," Jake begged. "Don't make me sleep beside Mariah. I've had to sleep with her every night for the last week. Don't make me sleep with her tonight."

Gen. Lee looked at Jake in disbelief. "Son, do you know how many men in this camp would trade their horse and saddle to have your problem? But whatever you want. I'll see you at breakfast."

In the morning they sat with General Lee and General Robert Hoke as they outlined their plan. "Hoke will take his troops and head toward Plymouth," Lee told them. "I can't spare him for long as I need him here in Virginia for the summer campaign.

"The beauty of this plan," he leaned toward them and dropped his voice to a whisper, "and this information must not leave this tent, is that for the first time we will use our ironclad steamer, the CSS Albemarle for support. We need to rid the North Carolina coast of those Yankees once and for all."

They bid Gen. Lee good-by. Again he kissed

Mariah's cheek. "You are brave, Mariah," he said. "Both you and Jake. Pray God we meet again in happier times."

Chapter 3

Mariah and Jake began their journey home. Their horses had needed the long night's rest. They, too, felt the unrest of the ravages of war—spooking at the sounds of distant cannon and gunshot. Their owners sensed that the animals were ready to be home in their familiar stables.

"We'll stay with the same people we stayed with on the way up," Mariah told Jake. "Everyone will be impressed that we actually talked with Gen. Lee."

"True," Jake agreed. "But we shouldn't say too much—especially about his plan to march to Plymouth. You heard what Cousin Bennie said about traitors among us."

"Oh, Jake, surely not. None of those people we stayed with would betray us."

Jake didn't answer, but appeared deep in thought. Mariah had come to respect the taciturn man during their time together. She reflected that Jake was brave and resourceful. He saw no need for idle conversation.

Mariah had been correct in her belief that their hosts wanted to know about their meeting with Gen. Lee. "What was he like?" they asked. "What did he say?"

She told them about her observation that the war had aged the handsome General. But she did not tell them about his plans. Not a whit.

Their last stop was in Benson, North Carolina. "We'll be home tomorrow," Jake said. "It'll sure be good to see my brothers again. I can't wait to tell them Cousin Bennie is alive."

They rode into the Alcorn homestead at dusk. Immediately they noticed that a pitchfork was not by the front gate. "Strange," Mariah remarked to Jake. "Should we go in or bypass this place?"

"No, I've known the Alcorns for years. They're a strange lot, but they're loyal. We won't mention the pitchfork, though. Let's see what unfolds. Maybe someone needed it to bale hay."

The Alcorns welcomed them warmly. They showed them their pitchfork badges and were as anxious to hear about their trip as everyone else had been. Mariah followed Jake's advice and didn't mention the missing pitchfork by the front gate.

"So you saw Gen. Lee?" Nancy Alcorn bellowed. "You actually saw him? What an honor."

Mariah had never liked Nancy. She was loud and bossy, ordering her husband around and always wanting her way. Mariah had no reason to feel this way, she just did.

"What did he say?" Nancy demanded. "What's his plan? He must have a plan based on your information."

"We can't share that, Nancy," Jake told her. "Gen. Lee asked us not to."

"Humph!" she snorted. "We risk our lives for the service of the Confederacy and Gen. Lee doesn't trust us enough to tell us what's going on? It's not right." For the rest of the evening she continually tried to wheedle information from her visitors.

Finally she gave up and offered them a drink to help them sleep. "Bottoms up," she encouraged. "It's ale we brew right here on the farm. It'll help you relax and tomorrow you can be on your way."

"Don't mind if I do," Jake said before downing a large gulp. Mariah took a few sips to be polite, but only wanted to go to bed. She had a horrible headache that she wanted to ease.

Around midnight Mariah woke with intense stomach cramps. But there was something else. Outside the window, high in the pines, a red-tailed hawk was screeching. "Kree-eee-ar. Kree-eee-ar. Kree-eee-ar." Three shrieks, then silence. In a few minutes, the screeches began again.

"Dang bird," she muttered. "Won't let a body sleep." But she knew she'd better hurry to the privy or the bed she and Jake shared would be soiled with the contents of her stomach and he would be furious.

Jake didn't stir when she shifted off the bed. That was strange. He'd proven to be a light sleeper and sensitive to any movement on her part.

He slept flat on his back in peaceful oblivion to her woes and to the bird's screams. He seemed even deader to the world than usual—almost as if he'd been drugged.

Drugged. Had Nancy drugged us? The ale she gave us was bitter. Maybe that's why Jake slept so soundly while my stomach wretched.

She ran out the back door to the privy, reaching it just in time. The hawk continued its shrieks. If anything, it had become more insistent with its raucous scream.

As she was leaving to go back to the house, she noticed three torches circling the yard. Strange. Why would anyone be out this time of night?

"Find her! She's got to be out here somewhere. Look in the privy." The unmistakable gruffness of Nancy Alcorn's voice giving orders to her husband and hired man stopped Mariah as she peered through a tall hedge.

"Aw, Nan," Billy Alcorn pleaded. "Mariah ain't never harmed us. Why you want to go and kill her?"

"You know what Thad Abrams said. There'll be no gold without bodies. Killing Jake was easy. Now find the girl."

"Miz Mariah, Miz Mariah, come quick. You ain't got much time." Mariah saw Sassy, the Alcorn's housekeeper, peering at her from the shadows. "Come quick to my cabin," she hissed.

Not knowing what else to do, Mariah turned and followed Sassy down the dirt path. There was no moon and it was dark as swamp water. She held onto Sassy's arm and followed her, fingering her throat and the birthmark as she went.

Inside the cabin Sassy shoved aside a braided rug and lifted a trap door. "Get in," she ordered. "Be quick."

"Why, Sassy. You're part of the Underground Railroad, aren't you?"

"Yessum, I am. And you better be glad this tunnel is here. They mean to kill you."

Mariah scurried into the hole and listened as Sassy replaced the rug. She could hear the corn shucks on Sassy's bed rustle as she climbed back into it.

Moments later her door banged opened and Nancy Alcorn was shouting at her. "Where is she, wench? Where have you hidden Mariah Long?"

Sassy did a wonderful imitation of someone who'd just been awakened from a sound sleep. "Wha—who you looking for, Miz Alcorn? Miz Mariah? Last time I seen her was at supper."

"You're lying! Nancy turned to her husband, "Search the cabin. She has to be here somewhere." Mariah could hear dishes breaking and a chair overturning as the Alcorns ransacked Sassy's home. But they didn't find the trap door.

Finally, they left. Sassy crawled back in bed and

Mariah huddled under the scratchy blanket that had been used by other fugitives before her. As her breath slowed to normal and her heart stopped racing she realized the woods were now quiet. The red tailed hawk had finally stopped screeching.

The next morning Mariah heard Sassy moving above her. She pulled aside the rug and opened the trap door. "You can come out, Miz Mariah. Theys all left. I heard them ride out during the night."

Mariah eased out of the tunnel, her muscles stiff from being cramped in the tight quarters. What had Nancy Alcorn shouted as she had raged last night? They had killed Jake? Could that be true?

The two women cautiously approached the house, but all was quiet—no rooster crowed, no dog barked. Once inside they saw evidence of the hasty retreat. Dirty dishes from last night were still on the table. The tankards Jake and Mariah had drunk from sat where they had left them. Too late Mariah realized none of the Alcorns had joined them in drinking the ale.

A blood-chilling scream reverberated from the back of the house. Sassy was peering into the room Jake and Mariah had shared.

"Don't go in there, Miz Mariah." She grabbed Mariah's arm to stop her, but Mariah pulled away and went in anyway.

There, on the bed where she had slept just a few hours before, lay Jake Wilton. He was covered in blood and excrement; his mouth gaped open. Through his chest, standing straight up from his body, was a pitchfork.

Mariah's stomach churned and she ran to the sink, gagging on what little bile she had left from the night before. Then she groped her way to the kitchen table and sat immobile. She heard Sassy in the other room humming sadly. She assumed her friend was cleaning up Jake's body. Her shoulders slumped forward. Jake had been her co-worker for a long time and she was shaken to the core.

Eventually Sassy came and joined Mariah. "I tried to warn you, Miz Mariah. I moved the pitchfork away from the front gate. That was all I could do. Mr. Abrams visited here several times and I heard their plans. No one thinks a darkie woman has sense enough to know what's going on."

"Thank you, Sassy. You saved my life. I just wish Jake and I had been more careful. He shouldn't have died so horrible a death but…." She could say no more. She knew the bloody scene of his murder would play through her mind for years to come.

Two brave women—one black, the other white, sat in silence while Mariah continued her musings. This is the end of The Group, she thought, because we don't know who we can trust.

Guess I'll go back to Brunswick County and continue teaching. I felt so guilty about leaving my students. They are good children. What did they think when they came to the schoolhouse and I wasn't there? School offered them a diversion from their dreary, poverty stricken lives.

And Pa. As hard as he is to live with, I know he loves me. He must have been worried that I left with no explanation. He guessed I aided the war effort. Many times he heard me complain about how much I hate the Yankees who disrupted my plans to further my education.

Finally, Sassy broke the silence. "You got one more duty, Miz Mariah. You got to take Jake back to his folks. I cleaned him up best as I could. I'll help you get him on his horse."

Between them, they dragged Jake's body across the yard and maneuvered him onto his horse's back. The beast seemed to know he had a sacred duty as the usually feisty animal stood absolutely still.

"Come with me, Sassy,' Mariah said. "I'll help you make a life. I owe you."

"You don't owe me nothing, Miz Mariah. I'se just glad those Alcorns is gone and you is alive. You was always kind to me. But I must stay here. I be awright. They'll be others coming through what need my hiding place."

Mariah mounted Lucy and began her journey back to the Wilton farm. She would arrive by nightfall with the sad news that their youngest brother was dead.

Hawk
Chapter 4

"Dang saw!" Hawk threw the dull instrument down in disgust and reached for his knife. He cut through the rest of the flesh and tossed the boy's leg onto the floor with other amputated limbs. The stench of pus and decay choked him as he tied off blood vessels and teased angry skin over the raw leg bone.

This cadet would live. Hawk was certain. Although he lay on the table, comatose from pain and trauma, he would survive. He was young—that was in his favor. But the telling fact was that maggots had been gnawing in the wound before the amputation. The boy had been waiting two days for treatment. Worms had eaten out most of the rot.

"Private, see to this man. I've got to get out of here."

"But Captain Hawkins, you can't leave now! There are three more men waiting."

Hawk pushed past the private and left the tent.

"Babies," he murmured to himself as he strode

across the yard. "They're just babies. That kid should be home helping his mother put up beans out of the garden."

Hawk let his six-foot frame sag against a tree and began to smoke his pipe. Sometimes that calmed him, sometimes it didn't. He was tired—tired of this war, tired of the blood and carnage, tired of telling boys barely old enough to shave that they'd never dance with a girl.

He lowered his head and tried to pray, but nothing came. God had forgotten him and these poor fools who were still fighting this endless war.

"Hawk, what happened in there? You can't just walk out of surgery."

Major James Richfield, Hawk's commanding officer, placed his hand on the surgeon's shoulder and forced him to look up.

"I've had it, Major. I'm sick of cutting on men who either die or are sent back to fight. That cadet whose leg I just cut off was nineteen-years-old. What kind of life will he have now?"

"He'll have a life, Hawk. Without you he'd be dead."

"I can't take it anymore. I've got to have a break from all this misery."

"Well, for better or worse, you're going to get one. We're pulling out. Thanks to the help of the cadets from the Virginia Military Institute, we beat old Franz Sigel and the Yankees here at New Market. We've forced the Yanks out of the Shenandoah Valley."

"But we can't just leave these kids," Hawk argued, in spite of himself.

"Local doctors can finish up. Lee wants us back in Northern Virginia. It's May. He'll begin his summer campaign soon."

Two days later, Hawk was ready to go. He checked on the VMI cadet whose leg he had amputated. The boy was propped up in bed playing cards with other soldiers.

"So you're the sawbones who took off my leg," the boy shouted. "Thanks, Doc, you saved my life."

"Aren't you bitter?" Hawk asked. "You'll go through the rest of your life with one leg."

"Are you joking? I'm going to get lots of sympathy from the young ladies back home. Think about it. If I'm dancing with one and happen to stumble and fall against her breast—well, it can't be helped, you know."

"Youth," Hawk muttered under his breath. Still, he was glad to see the lad up and about and determined to find a way to dance with girls.

As he was saddling his horse for the long ride, Major Richfield approached and handed him a sheaf of papers. "New orders, Hawk, you're not going with us."

"What? Can't the Army make up its mind?"

"This is straight from Major General Breckenridge. Though I must say I mentioned your name for the assignment."

Hawk rifled through the papers. "I'm heading south instead of north? But I thought we were supposed to join Lee."

"General Grant has been given command of the entire Union Army. He's appointed some upstart— Sherman is his name—to replace him as head of the Western Theater. Our scouts tell us Sherman plans to invade Georgia to counteract Lee in Northern Virginia. Breckenridge wants you to go south and join General Joseph Johnston and the Army of the Tennessee."

"So why did you mention my name? Doesn't Lee need surgeons in his army?"

"Frankly, Hawk. You need a change. I'm worried you're going to crack under pressure. I don't think Sherman will amount to much, but you never know.

"Go south. Maybe stop by and see your folks in North Carolina. Try to meet up with Johnston by the end of May."

"Is anyone going with me?"

"Yes, Private Jones who helps you in surgery. Then you're to choose two others. But you're the commanding officer."

"I'll take Lieutenant Nance and Private Barnes. They're good men and know how to assist in the operating room."

Chapter 5

Hawk and his party left early the next morning. His plan was to head south to Tarboro, N.C., stay a few days, maybe a week, and then join Gen. Johnston in South Carolina or Georgia.

He knew his mother and youngest sister would be thrilled with this unexpected visit. His mother would cook more food than they could ever eat. He wished he could see his father, but he had been killed at Chickamauga.

Jones and Barnes better not flirt with Brie, he thought. I'll kill them if they even look her in the eye. He wasn't worried about Nance. The man had never shown interest in women. Hawk had always wondered why.

The men rode at leisure. After months of the stress of battle they enjoyed springtime in the foothills.

They rode into the Hawkins' farm at sunset on the fourth day of their journey. Hawk sat back in his saddle and admired the homestead before entering the gate. Built by his grandfather in 1830, the farmhouse had withstood storms, droughts, and family crises. Its wide porch covered with low-slung roof had welcomed visitors and bid farewell to caskets on their way to the cemetery.

Brie was in the front yard chasing a recalcitrant pig. "Get on, pig," she shrieked. "Get back in that pen." Hawk dismounted and hurried to help his sister.

"Wha...?" Brie stammered as the tall man entered her space and swatted the squealing animal.

She turned and ran into the house. "Mama!" she shouted. "There are men in the yard. They're trying to steal our pig!"

Annabelle Hawkins came onto the porch with a raised shotgun. She lowered it when the tall man stretched out his hands and came toward her. "Hello, Mama," Hawk whispered when he was near. "You're as beautiful as I remember."

"Hawk," she murmured, then repeated, "Hawk."

Hawk enfolded his mother in a bear hug. Brie joined them, throwing her arms around her brother's neck. "I'm sorry, Hawk," she cried. "I thought you were trying to steal Wally. He's the last pig we've got."

Annabelle broke Hawk's embrace and cradled his face as she had when he was eight-years-old. She searched his coffee brown eyes for answers to every mother's questions.

Hawk heard the edgy rustling of men and horses behind him. Turning, he signaled for his men to come forward. After tying their horses to a fence, Barnes, Jones, and Nance came for introductions.

"Stay," Annabelle insisted. "Stay with us as long as you can. Have you eaten tonight?"

"We haven't," Hawk answered. "I've been telling the boys what a great cook you are and we're famished. Have you got any fried chicken or maybe a slab of bacon and some biscuits?"

Annabelle looked at her son in astonishment, and then turned and walked into her house.

"Come on, boys," Hawk told his men. "Let's put our horses in the barn then wash up. You're in for a treat tonight!"

Thirty minutes later Annabelle served the soldiers turnip soup and hoe cakes. Brie set tankards of well water at each man's place. Hawk stared at the stringy turnips floating in his bowl, and then raised his eyes to his mother.

"Mama?"

"It's the best we have, son." Annabelle jutted out her chin in defiance of circumstances she could not control. "Brie was telling the truth. Wally is our last pig. I have two laying hens but we won't eat them until we must. We need the eggs."

In spite of the meager food, the men enjoyed sitting at table with Hawk's family. Lt. Nance entertained with stories from his childhood. Growing up on a farm in eastern Virginia had subjected him to summers of working in the tobacco fields.

"One summer I was in charge of driving Bertie, our mule, in the 'baccy field. I would guide as she pulled the 'baccy sled down the rows so our hands could pick the leaves and throw them on. One day Paw told me to hold up; the hands weren't ready. So I tied Bertie to a tree and crawled under a bush out of the sun and fell asleep. When I woke up Paw was hollering at Bertie and beating her with a stick. She had gotten loose and eaten half a row of 'baccy. When he got through beating the mule, he took the stick to me. I've still got bruises from that day." Nance rubbed his backside for emphasis.

Hawk couldn't help but notice the shy glances Pvt. Jones shared with his sister. At sixteen Brie, short for Sabrina, was a beauty. Her eyes, brown like his but deeper and larger, and her long blonde curls, were alluring.

Hawk sat on the porch with his mother long after the others had gone to bed. "Tell me the truth, Mama," he ventured. "How are you and Brie getting by? I had no idea things were so bad. We're pretty well fed in the Army, though I have heard of shortages."

"It's hard, son. I won't lie to you. We'll survive. I grew up poor; I know how to manage. Your sister Julia who's married to Pastor Brown helps us. The church people give them their excess—apples from an abundant crop, huckleberries they've picked—that sort of thing. It's not easy."

"But why? This farm produced everything we needed when we were growing up."

Annabelle sighed. "Several reasons. Everyone is in a bad way, son. We've had drought—it hasn't rained in a month. Soldiers come riding through and take what we have—not just Yankees; Confederates are just as bad.

"Also, there are no men to work the fields. The few that are left are either too old, in diapers, or maimed from the war. We women do what we can, but it's not enough."

Hawk slammed his fist into his palm. "This cussed war! When will it end? Why does the Lord Jesus let it drag on and on? I don't want to leave you and Brie in this sorry state."

"I don't expect you to stay, Hawk. You have a duty to your commanding officers and to the soldiers who need you. I do expect you to keep your faith, though, and not take the Lord's name in vain. This war drags on because of man's pride, stubbornness, and greed. The Lord Jesus must cry just as we do.

"I raised you in the faith. There will be times when that's all that will sustain you. Do you still have the pocket Bible I gave you when you joined the Army?"

Hawk reached inside his shirt and produced a small, well-worn book. "I try to read it, Mama, I do. Sometimes I find answers; most of the time I don't."

Annabelle took her son's hand and caressed it in the darkness. There was nothing more to say.

The men stayed for three days. Major Richfield had said they could take their time, but Hawk knew the war was reaching a climax. Also, he was reluctant to continue eating his mother's store of food.

They rode out of the gate on Thursday, May 25th. Hawk noted the date, remembering that a mere ten days earlier he had amputated the cadet's leg during the Battle of New Market. He breathed a quick prayer for the boy, and then turned to wave to his mother and sister.

As they rode down the drive, away from the house, Pvt. Jones eased his horse beside Hawk's. "Captain," he stammered, head bent into his collar, "when this war is over would you mind, well, I mean, could I...?"

"What, Jones? Could you what? Spit it out, man."

"Could I call on your sister? She's the most beautiful woman I've ever seen and it would make me happy to get to know her and I think she liked me and I..."

"Shut up, boy. You're babbling like a baby. Call on Brie, you say?" Hawk looked at the sniveling boy, but realized he had come to like him and that he would mature into a trustworthy man.

"Well, I'll have to think on that," Hawk answered. "I'll just have to think on that."

Waddell
Chapter 6

"What's your plan, Hawk?" Lt. Nance asked riding up beside him.

"Our orders are to meet Gen. Johnston. We'll go to Camp Magnum in Raleigh. Someone there will know where Johnston is."

They arrived at the camp in mid-afternoon. "I remember coming here to train when I joined the Army," Pvt. Barnes told the others. "We were all spit and polish. Thought we'd go home in a few months. Look at these poor blokes. They know what's coming and they're not happy."

"Gen. Johnston is in north Georgia," the camp commander told them. "Scouts passed through here yesterday on their way to report to President Davis in Richmond.

"There's heavy fighting around Cartersville. Sherman is pushing toward Atlanta and Johnston hasn't been able stop him."

"We were told Sherman wasn't much of a threat," Hawk said.

"Tell that to the people in Atlanta. I hear they're leaving the city like rats off a sinking ship."

"Then we'll leave at first light. With your permission we'll stock up on provisions and give our horses a good night's rest."

Hawk and his men were on the road as the sun rose over Walnut Creek. "We can join Johnston in five days—six at the most," Hawk said. "But we'll have to push."

Three days into their ride they were approaching Greenville, South Carolina. The soldiers had ridden hard and encountered few people on the road until three ragged Confederates stopped them and asked for water. The dirty men stumbled along the dusty road leading a goat.

"We're going home," they told Hawk's party. "We were with Gen. Johnston at Cassville. We got our tails whipped because Gen. Hood didn't attack as ordered."

"You're deserting?" Lance asked in amazement. Don't you know Governor Vance has ordered all deserters shot?"

"He'll have to catch me first," the obvious ringleader scoffed. "And my woman will hide me under her warm nightie."

The other two marauders laughed at their comrade's bawdy joke, punching each other and nodding in agreement. These two appeared dimwitted and content to follow their leader's control.

Hawk noticed fresh blood stains across one man's shirt and wondered about the truth of their story.

"Why do you have a goat?" he questioned. "Does Gen. Johnston give a free goat to everyone who deserts?"

"We found it wandering by the road. Thought I'd take it home and start me a goat herd," the leader answered. "Or maybe we'll roast goat steaks for supper."

More laughing and more punching from the two sidekicks. "Let's go, boys," he said. "I think I hear my woman calling and I'm ready!"

"Deserters," Hawk growled as he watched them leave. "Dirty, rotten deserters. I have no use for such filth."

"What's that smoke behind those trees?" Jones asked as they resumed their journey. "We're not in Georgia yet."

As the men rounded a grove of pecan trees they reined their horses in sharply and stared. Before them lay the shell of a small cabin smoldering to the ground.

The breeze blew hot ashes in their faces and something more horrific. The battle-hardened men knew the stench of burning flesh. Two fly infested, mutilated bodies—a man and a woman—lay before them, gaping hollow-eyed at the sky.

"Damn," Barnes breathed, the bile rising in his throat. "Look at that."

"Those deserters," snarled Hawk. "They did this."

"Hawk—they're Negroes," Jones said. "The deserters killed coloreds."

"Doesn't matter. They were human beings and murder is murder. We've got to bury them before we go on."

The soldiers dismounted and led their horses back to the pecan trees. "Tie them up and let them rest," Hawk said. "Jones, do you still have that camp shovel in your backpack?"

Jones pulled out the shovel and handed it to Hawk. Then the men tied kerchiefs around their faces for protection.

"Where shall we bury them, Hawk?" Lance asked.

"How about under the pecan trees? It's a pretty spot."

The men split into pairs and picked up the bodies. "These folks haven't been dead long," Hawk said. "They're not stiff yet."

"Billy, Bill-ee. Come here, Billy. Where is you, Billy?" The men stood gripping the bodies and stared as a young black boy came stumbling toward them from behind the ruined cabin. "Billy. Where is you, Billy?"

When the boy got to the soldiers he asked, "Is you seed Billy? He's my goat and I can't find him."

Hawk set the dead man's feet on the ground and knelt beside the boy. "Who are you, son?"

"Where's Billy? I'se got to git him in the barn afore

Pa whups me."

Hawk looked at the child. He was slight, almost frail; but his eyes were intelligent. They were the eyes of one who had seen true evil. He obviously belonged to the man and the woman they were going to bury. The boy's eyes were unfocused and his entire body twitched.

"Who are you, son?" Hawk asked. This time he put his hands on the boy's face and forced him to make eye contact.

The boy shook his head twice. The glazed eyes cleared and looked deeply into Hawk's own. "Waddell," he answered. "I'se Waddell. Ise ten years old. Is you seed Billy?"

"What's your last name, Waddell? And what happened here?"

"Waddell. That's my name. Waddell Waddell. Pa said it be a good name so they used it twice."

"Where's your Pa, Waddell?"

The boy lowered his gaze and pointed to the dead man. "That's Pa. His name is Waddell. And that's Ma," he said, shifting his focus.

Hawk couldn't resist. "Is her name Waddell, too?"

The child looked at Hawk as if he'd lost his mind. "No, 'course not. Her name is Alice. Alice Waddell."

"What happened here, Waddell?" Jones asked, coming up behind the boy and putting a hand on his shoulder. "Who did this to your people?"

"Three white men. Three soldiers. I was walking

home from Granny's and I seed them come up to the cabin. I hid in the trees cause I was skart. They beat on the door and when Pa opened it they grabbed him and drug him out in the yard. Then one man went back inside. I heard a gun go off. They must've shot my little brother Will, cause when they came out they only had Ma. They threw her on the ground and the men got on her and they… and they…"

Waddell could say no more. He doubled at the waist and choked out great, gulping sobs.

Jones put his arms around the boy and held him. "It'll be all right, son," he crooned as tenderly as a mother comforting a sick child. "Let us bury your Ma and Pa, then we'll help you."

Waddell sniffed loudly, then leaned against Jones. "Does you know where Billy is? I raised him from a baby."

Jones squeezed the boy's shoulders. "I'm afraid the men who killed your family took Billy. We met them on the road. We didn't know what they had done."

Hawk joined them and released Waddell from Jones' embrace. "We were going to bury your parents in the trees," he said. "Is that all right with you?"

Waddell furrowed his brow. "Yes," he agreed. "That would be awright. Ma loved sitting under the trees. Said it was her 'thinking place'."

Hawk and his men watched with amazement as Waddell helped bury his parents. As they patted the last shovel of dirt on his father's grave, Waddell said he wanted to pray.

"My dad is the preacher at Waddell A.M.E. Church," he reasoned. "Sometimes he lets me preach. Says I'm his 'ssistant. That makes me a preacher, too."

"You should pray, son," Hawk agreed. "Take off your caps and bow your heads boys," he told his men.

"Lord," Waddell began. "This be my ma and pa whose coming up to you. They's good people. They never hurt no one. Take them home, Lord. Receive them into your bosom and give them rest.

"And Lord, bless those men what done this. Show them sin ain't no way to live. Save them from the fiery pit, Lord, and forgive them."

Four grown men who had seen sights too horrible to talk about, gaped at the child as he forgave the men who had raped his mother and murdered his people.

"How can you pray for their forgiveness, Waddell?" Barnes asked. "They killed your mother, brother, and father."

"They's God's chillum no matter what they done. God will deal with them as need be. But He loves them jest the same. That's why I gots to pray for their souls."

"What are you going to do now, Waddell?" Hawk asked as they left the new cemetery. "Can we take you somewhere? How about that Granny you were visiting."

"She ain't my granny. She a witch. She gives us potions and stuff when we be sick. That's why I was at her cabin. Pa's got a wart on his foot that's driving him crazy and Granny gave me some…" Waddell stopped. "I guess that old wart won't bother Pa no more."

"But maybe you can stay with her until you find your people."

"I ain't gonna stay with Granny. She's got spiders and snakes in her cabin, and creepy things in jars. I'se skart of Granny. And I ain't got no people. You'se my people now."

"You can't go with us, Waddell. We're going to join Gen. Johnston in Georgia. That's where the fighting is. I can't take you there."

Waddell stuck out his chin, planted his feet, and crossed his arms. "I'se going with you. I can cook your food and brush your horses. You'se my people now."

"Let's take him as far as Greenville," Lance suggested. "We can leave him at a Negro church. Someone there will know what to do."

"All right, Hawk agreed. But only as far as Greenville." He mounted his horse then leaned down and hoisted Waddell's slight body up behind him.

Hawk and his soldiers had lost several hours stopping to bury the Waddells. They rode until after dark to make up lost time.

Waddell kept his word. He leaped off Hawk's horse and soon had a fire blazing. Rummaging through the men's saddlebags he found food and utensils to make a meal. While the men ate, he brushed and fed the horses.

"He's good, Hawk," Barnes said. "Maybe we should keep him."

Hawk bristled. "We are not taking a ten-year-old to war. Forget it."

After dinner the men rolled out their sleeping gear. Exhausted, they didn't care that the ground was hard. Waddell had no gear.

"Can I sleep beside you, Mr. Hawk?" he asked. "I'se sort of missing Ma and Pa. Sure would make me feel better."

Hawk had no choice. He spread out his bedding and indicated where the boy should lie, and then lay down beside him. Jones, Barnes, and Lance snickered as Waddell threw his arm across Hawk's chest and snuggled into the curve of his body. "You'se my people now, Mr. Hawk. Yes, you is," he whispered before he fell asleep.

Hawk lay awake long and watched the sliver of a new moon climb high into the night sky. Waddell tossed and turned by his side, often whimpering and crying out for his ma or pa. How could people be so cruel, he wondered. Murdering a whole family?

Toward morning he snuggled the child into the crook of his arm, and they both slept.

The soldiers were up at first light. Waddell wanted to cook breakfast but Hawk was firm. "We can eat hardtack as we ride. We need to make good time today."

The men decided to take turns carrying Waddell so

that no horse would be overly tired. They soon found another reason to share the boy's company. Waddell was a talker. For men used to riding long hours without conversation, this soon became an annoyance.

Most of the time Waddell quoted from the Bible. He could name all of the books of both the Old Testament and the New Testament in chronological order. He could recite the books of the New Testament backwards. "I'm trying to learn to do that with the Old Testament," he told Lance as he clutched the man's waist. "It's hard, but I'll do it. Wanna hear what I can do so far?"

Lance groaned but didn't answer. He knew it would make no difference.

Around noon, the men saw a dust cloud on the horizon. Soon a lone Confederate soldier appeared, whipping his horse to breakneck speed. Reluctantly, the rider pulled up when he reached Hawk's party.

"Hold on, friend, "Hawk shouted. "Where are you going in such a hurry? You'll kill your horse if you don't slow down."

"Can't," the rider gasped. "Got to get word to headquarters. Gen. Johnston needs reinforcements, and he needs them now."

"That's where we're going," Hawk told him. "We were told that Johnston is near Cassville, Ga."

"Johnston has left Cassville. He stalled Sherman at New Hope Church and Pickett's Mill, but that fox outmaneuvered him and is twenty miles from Atlanta."

The messenger shouted the last over his shoulder as he spurred his horse forward.

"What are we going to do, Hawk?" Jones asked.

"Turn south and find Gen. Johnston. That's our orders. Waddell will have to come with us. We'll think of something to do with him when we get there."

McAllister
Chapter 7

"Stupid cook!" Jacob McAllister threw his breakfast in the dirt and stomped on it with his boot. "How can anyone eat that slop? I wouldn't feed it to a pig."

"That's enough, Lieutenant," Brigadier General Henry Wessells reprimanded. "Quit being a baby. You're not at your Mama's dinner table. Now get ready to move out. I need information on what the Johnny Rebs are doing."

McAllister grimaced, ashamed to be corrected by the General. That was no way to earn a promotion. "Yes sir," he answered smartly. "What's my assignment?"

Wessels handed him a set of written orders. "I want you to scout the Wilmington to Weldon railroad. We've got to break that supply line. Lee calls it the lifeline of the Confederacy. Ever since the Rebs took back Plymouth, they've been flaunting their presence in eastern North Carolina. I still don't understand how Lee knew that Plymouth would not be well fortified in mid-April and was able to send Gen. Hoke to retake the town. It was a great loss for us since Plymouth is at the mouth of the Roanoke River."

"That was a major blow, sir," McAllister agreed, ignoring the fact that he'd played a significant role in the defeat by passing information to Mariah Long.

"You're many things, McAllister," Wessells continued, "but you're an expert scout. We're close to Weldon. Start there. That's the distribution point for goods to Lee's army. From there, supplies go to Petersburg, Richmond, and the Army of Northern Virginia. Follow the railroad to Wilmington. It's the last port that's open for the Confederates. It's where the blockade runners bring goods in from Europe.

"Find the weak links in the supply line. Find where they're vulnerable. That's where we'll attack."

"Um, General, how about my promotion to captain?" McAllister asked.

"We'll see how you perform on this assignment—then maybe a promotion."

McAllister went to his tent and opened his trunk. Moving aside personal items, he reached to the bottom and pulled out the uniform taken off a dead Confederate private. The soldier couldn't have been more than eighteen-years-old.

"Too bad, kid," McAllister had sneered at the corpse as he stripped off the pants. "You won't need these anymore."

He had soaked the uniform in cold water for three days before the bloodstains came out. When he finished, it was more tattered than ever. "That's good," McAllister had muttered. "I'll look like I've been in heavy fighting."

He changed quickly and left without speaking to anyone. Few people knew he was a scout. He liked the freedom of movement and being on his own. In addition to the uniform, he had worked hard to develop the persona of a Confederate soldier. He had even taken diction lessons to develop a Southern accent.

Since he was traveling alone, he could make good time. His plan was to skirt other soldiers—both Confederate and Union—as much as possible. If stopped he was prepared. He carried two sets of identification. One was his orders from Gen. Wessells. The other was counterfeit orders for a Confederate soldier to join Gen. Whiting at Ft. Fisher, North Carolina.

As Gen. Wessells suggested, he started in Weldon, located in northeastern North Carolina. Although the town was small, it was a bustle of activity. McAllister rode through the dusty streets and marveled at the supplies being loaded onto railroad cars. He had not realized that the Confederates were still transporting so many goods up from Wilmington.

After a few well placed inquiries, he learned that there were nine Confederate training camps in and around Weldon. He could not advise Wessells to attack here.

McAllister left Weldon and headed south toward Wilmington. All along the railroad he found well guarded, carefully patrolled tracks. The Confederates knew that this railroad was vital to the survival of their cause.

Traveling through Rocky Mount, Wilson, and Goldsboro, McAllister saw no weak link for Gen. Wessells to exploit.

His luck changed in tiny Willard, North Carolina. The crossroads was located on the swampy, snake-infested banks of the Cape Fear River in Pender County. Three young Confederates were guarding the depot.

"Afternoon, boys. Seen any Yankees?" McAllister called from his horse.

The soldiers looked up from their card game and grinned. "That's right funny," a freckled, red headed boy laughed. "Ain't no Yankees 'round here. The Yankees is scared. We chased them off in Plymouth and they ain't coming back."

"Yeah," another soldier echoed. "Yankees ain't gonna bother with this hole. Ain't nothing here but mosquitoes, snakes and some railroad tracks. We see maybe one train a day go through here. Those boys on the train just wave and keep going."

"Who's your commanding officer?" McAllister asked after he had dismounted and approached the Rebs. "I've got news from Gen. Whiting."

More laughter from the soldiers. "You mean old

Capt. Hardy?" the third soldier snickered. "He's in town. You can talk to him tomorrow—if he can get his nose out of the bottle and stumble back to camp."

McAllister joined in the laughter. "Yeah, some officers are pretty bad. What would the Army be without enlisted men?"

"Aren't you sort of old to be a private?" the redhead asked, cocking his head toward McAllister.

"What can I say?" McAllister fenced. "I was on the road to promotion but the General's daughter sort of liked me, you know what I mean? That old cuss blamed me because I had her in the bushes with her skirts up. I was just giving the lady what she wanted."

"I like you," the second young Confederate said. "Why don't you bunk with us tonight? My name's James. I'm from Kinston. These here are my buddies. Joe has that awful red hair, and the one with the big nose, well, we just call him Snoot."

"Don't mind if I do," McAllister agreed. "I could use the company."

As the night wore on McAllister learned that the Confederates could provide more than companionship. Joe was from the mountains of North Carolina and came from a family adept at making moonshine. The four men drank whiskey and played cards late into the evening.

McAllister was careful to limit his drinking and made certain to end the evening as the winner at cards. He wanted to be invited to stay longer. The boys were typical of young soldiers he had known in the Union Army—brash, cocky, and amateurs at poker.

By midnight the Confederates were snoring on their cots. McAllister counted his winnings and then explored his surroundings.

The outpost consisted of two tents adjacent to the railroad tracks. The men slept in one tent and the other was their base of operations. In the base tent was a wooden chair and a crude desk holding an old telegraph device. "Easy to take," McAllister muttered to himself.

As he left he heard a strange squawk coming from behind the base tent.

"What the...?" McAllister cried as he rounded the tent and collided with a large cage. From inside the cage a majestic bird glared at him with hatred as it continued to make throaty, guttural noises.

"Who, or what are you?" he asked.

The creature fell silent but continued eyeing McAllister through hooded, malevolent eyes. The bird had dark brown feathers on its back, fading to lighter brown on its breast. Its yellow talons and curved beak proved it was a raptor. But its red tail made McAllister certain of its identity. "A red tailed hawk," he whispered. "Why would anyone cage such a beautiful bird?"

He stared at the bird a while longer and then left. He would ask the Confederates about the bird in the morning.

"That's my hawk," Snoot told him as they ate

breakfast. "It's a female. I found her last week tangled in some bushes down by the river. See my hands? She 'bout tore the skin off when I was catching her."

"What are you going to do with her? She's beautiful. Why don't you let her loose?"

"She's beautiful, all right. I'm going to take her to Wilmington the next time I go. There's a woman there who will pay well for her feathers. She uses them to make ladies hats. She even sells some of her creations to men—fancy men, that is."

"But they'll kill her. You can't let them kill her!" McAllister was self-centered and ruthless to people, but he was soft hearted about animals.

Snoot laughed. "It's just a bird. And I can use the money."

The day was a repetition of the previous evening— more drinking, more card playing, more boasting. Capt. Hardy never made an appearance.

Around one o'clock, a slow train from Wilmington clattered through the small outpost. It slowed for the boys to get their mail and throw their own mailbag aboard, then picked up speed as it headed for Goldsboro.

"That's it for today," James said. "Now let's get back to cards so I can win my money back."

Just as the night before, the young soldiers were passed out by midnight. McAllister had let them win back their money. He considered it small payment for the information he had gained.

He rolled up his pack and moved silently to where his horse was tethered. "I'll be right back, Blackie," he whispered to his gelding after he had saddled him. "I've got one more thing to do."

He sneaked behind the base tent to the hawk's cage. "Be quiet, my beauty," he whispered. "If you make noise we're both going to get our feathers plucked."

The bird seemed to understand. When McAllister stretched his arm into the cage she hopped onto his wrist. As he pulled his arm out he spoke softly to her. "Fly away, pretty girl. God grant you a long life and lots of baby hawks."

The bird lowered her head toward McAllister as if in thanks, and then spread her great wings and flew high into the nearest pine tree. She looked once more at the man who watched from below. As she flew into the night she sounded a triumphant "Kree-eee-ar."

"Oh, great," McAllister muttered to himself. "That's just what I need. She's calling her mate, now she'll wake the boys."

Chapter 8

Snoot turned over on his cot. A noise roused him. He tried to go back to sleep but he had drunk too much whiskey. He stumbled out of bed to relieve himself outside of the tent.

The other two Confederates slept soundly. "Where's the newcomer?" Snoot said into the darkness. Expecting to find McAllister outside, he was not concerned.

But he wasn't there. And his bedroll was gone. "James, Joe," Snoot shouted, trying to rouse his companions. "Wake up! We've been had!" Both were comatose. Snoot shook them and slapped their faces, but got no response.

A slow realization struck Snoot. "I know what that noise was," he muttered. "That jerk let my hawk loose." When he walked around the base tent, his fears were confirmed. The door of the empty cage mocked him as it swung on its hinges.

"Son of a..." he growled. "I'll kill him! I'll track

that creep down and I'll kill him."

McAllister knew that the hawk's screech might wake the Confederates. He leaped on Blackie and urged him into the woods. He had studied maps of the area but he was in unfamiliar territory. Soon, he was lost in the dark.

"We'll have to lay low until morning," he told his horse. "Then I can figure how to get us out of this mess." Leading the horse into a thicket of tall pines, he resigned himself to his situation.

"Ha! Thought you could escape, did you?" Snoot stepped from behind a large oak and laughed at his adversary. "I've been tracking you for the last twenty minutes. I know these parts and I know that you're lost. You're lucky you didn't wander into that swamp over there and get eaten by gators."

McAllister shrugged. There was nothing to say. He'd been bested.

"Why'd you let my hawk loose? That was none of your business."

McAllister shrugged again. He wasn't going to give the boy the satisfaction of an argument.

"You ain't one of us, is you? You ain't a Confederate. I used to spend summers with my aunt in New York. You hide it pretty good, but sometimes you talk just like them Yankees."

"Lt. Jacob McAllister, 12th Regiment, New York Calvary. Born and raised in Oswego County, New York

State."

"You're a lousy spy. You're spying on the railroad. I'm going to take you back and we'll send your lousy soul to Andersonville Prison. No. No, I'm not. You stole my hawk. I'm going to shoot you right….Agggh!"

McAllister's bullet ripped through Snoot's throat. The Rebel grabbed his neck and fell forward as blood spewed over his shirt.

The woods echoed from the shot—frogs stopped croaking, the hoot owl was silent, and the crickets ceased their incessant hum.

McAllister lowered his pistol. "You were a fool, Snoot. Nobody gets the drop on the best shot in the 12th Regiment. Now I've got to figure out what to do with your sorry body."

Daylight was edging through the woods. McAllister watched as pink streaks shot over the dark pines and outlined the swamp.

As soon as he was sure of his footing, he dragged Snoot's body to the muck and tossed it in. It slapped the water with a resounding splash, followed immediately by a second splash. McAllister knew that an alligator had caught its breakfast.

McAllister pulled out his crude map of the area. By now it was light enough to see that he wasn't far off the road. "Let's go on to Wilmington," he told Blackie. "I can scout the depot there and you can spend the night in a stable."

He rode into Wilmington in the early afternoon. He had visited the city before the war and thought it beautiful. What he found now was quite different.

Haggard soldiers walked the streets or sat idly in doorways. Many were missing limbs or had festering sores and wounds on their faces and arms. All wore tattered uniforms.

Stately homes still lined Market and Third Streets, but the air of privilege and grandeur was gone.

He made his way to Water Street and the river. A blockade runner was being unloaded at Chandler's Wharf. He watched as local merchants bid for the goods, amazed at the prices being offered.

"This cargo is for the Army," the captain shouted. "Lee needs this gunpowder and paper worse than you do." Still the haggling continued.

As McAllister left the docks and headed for the train depot, he noticed a post office among the government buildings. I should write to my sister Anne, he thought. She must be frantic since I haven't written for over a month.

He always carried stationary in the pouch strapped to his waist. An opportunity to post a letter was a godsend and he knew to be prepared. He leaned against an oak tree and wrote a quick note to his only sibling.

As he sealed the letter, he realized he had a problem. "How am I going to mail this?" he asked no one in particular. "They'll be questions when a stranger tries to post a letter to Oswego, New York."

He moved to a nearby bench to ponder his dilemma. Thirty minutes later he was no nearer a solution and decided he would wait until he was with his unit to send the letter.

Idly, he watched a pretty girl ascend the post office steps. She was dressed simply but had a certain air of purpose and confidence. Then he realized he knew her. "That's Mariah," he whispered. "Mariah Long—the spy."

While Mariah was in the post office, McAllister formed a plan. She'll mail this letter for me, he thought. Don't know how I'll convince her, but I've always been able to sweet-talk the ladies.

When Mariah came out, she descended the steps and turned in McAllister's direction. He could tell she was deep in thought.

"Hello, pretty lady," he said. "Fancy meeting you here."

Mariah jerked her head up at the sound of his voice—a voice she'd recognize anywhere. Instinctively, her hand flew to her birthmark.

"McAllister," was all she could say.

"Is that anyway to greet a friend? Especially someone who has done so much for you. You Rebs won at Plymouth because of information I gave you. Surely that deserves a hug and a kiss."

Mariah had regained her composure. "I'd rather kiss a pig than you, McAllister. You've got your nerve—

showing up in Wilmington dressed as one of ours."

"What can I say? I'm on assignment. And I have an assignment for you. I want you to post a letter to my sister in New York."

"Why in the world would I do that for you? I owe you no favors."

"Yes, you do. I've given you good information the last few years. And I have some more for you."

Mariah lowered her head and sighed. "We have no money. The gold has dried up. Most of our supporters have given up hope for our cause."

"That's too bad. I'm short on the bankroll I need to retire. However, you and I have too much on each other. If you turn me in, your main source of information dries up. If I expose you, you lose your cover and your ability to spy. So mail the letter."

Mariah grabbed the letter. "What if I raise the money? Where can I meet you to find out about this mission?"

"I'm leaving Wilmington today and going back to Plymouth. I have an assignment in Raleigh in two weeks. Wessells won't act on my information before then. If you want to know what I know, meet me at one o'clock at the Carolina Inn. I'll even buy you lunch."

Mariah glared at him, snatched the letter from his hand, and then turned to go back to the post office.

Three Lives Converge
Chapter 9

Mariah left Wilmington in a foul mood. McAllister had information, that was certain. Yet she had no money to pay him and no hope of raising it. He had given her two weeks, hardly time to raise the gold he demanded.

She drove the buggy the forty-five miles to her home. Lucy was a young horse and with frequent breaks, she could travel the distance. She had been stabled in Wilmington with Mariah's Aunt Tillie's mares for the last three nights, so she was well fed and rested. The early November sunshine energized her, but did nothing to lighten Mariah's mood.

"Is that you, Mariah? Where've you been so long, girl?" Pa hollered as soon as she came in the back door.

"I told you, Pa. I went to stay with Aunt Tillie for a few days. She lives by herself and gets lonely."

"I get lonely, too. Did you ever think about that? I'm your Pa. Tillie's just your old maid aunt."

"I know, Pa. I know." Mariah was too tired and too discouraged to argue. She knew that her pa hated her mother's only sister and that Tillie returned the sentiment. Mariah had long been in the middle of that feud.

Her pa wouldn't be appeased. "I haven't eaten since you left. I'm starving. And Mrs. Wilson came by and wanted to know when you would be back to teach her young'uns. Said they were driving her crazy."

Mariah could tell by the small pile of unwashed plates in the sink that Pa had not eaten well while she was gone. At least he had moved his dirty dishes off the table.

She sighed and moved on. "I told the children I'd be gone for a few days and gave them assignments to complete. Are you hungry? I'll cook something if you are."

"Nah, don't bother. If you're going off and leaving me to suffer, I can make it through one more evening."

"Then I'm going to bed. I'm tired."

"It's only eight o'clock. Are you sick?"

"No, Pa. I'm just tired. Tired to the bone."

Life returned to normal over the next week. Mariah went back to school and Pa remained querulous. Try as she might, she could think of no way to raise money for McAllister. Her mind was far from her duties, both at home and at school.

On the Sunday after she had seen McAllister, Mariah decided to go to church and ask for God's help. She sometimes skipped the service, but not often. Teachers were supposed to attend worship every Sunday to set an example.

She prayed for a way to raise the gold but got no answer. Dispirited, she trudged home to fix her pa's dinner.

"What's wrong with you, girl?" he grumbled as she ladled burned potatoes onto his plate. "Did that old witch Tillie say something to upset you? You haven't been the same since you came back from Wilmington."

Mariah had had enough. She was tired of Pa's griping and tired of her own worries. "No!" she shouted. "Tillie didn't upset me. Don't you think I have a life, Pa? Don't you think I have problems besides you, Tillie, and my students?"

She ran from the kitchen and threw herself onto a settee in the next room. She couldn't help it. Tears of frustration and discouragement burst forth and she cried with abandon.

Her pa, crotchety disagreeable alcoholic that he was, got up from his chair and came to her. He sat beside her and pulled her onto his lap as he had when she was ten-years-old.

"I know, sweetheart," he crooned brushing hair from her eyes and tears from her face. "I know you have worries. Tell me. Somehow you've gotten involved with this crazy war that's destroying all of us. Tell me your troubles."

Mariah told him—everything. She told him about meeting Gen. Lee, about The Group, about

Jake Wilton's death, about Betsy's rape. She told him about Jacob McAllister and her part in the victory at Plymouth. Then she told him that McAllister had more information, but that she had no money to pay for it.

"He said he'd be in Raleigh in two weeks, Pa. That was a week ago. He said he had new information if I could pay him. I can't. Sources that I had, people who thought we could win this war, are gone. Whatever McAllister has to say, I'll never know."

By now she was exhausted. She rested her head on her pa's shoulder and sniffled. Pa continued to stoke her hair and said nothing other than an occasional "Hm-m-m."

"I can give you gold, Mariah," he finally whispered. "I have a stash I've been saving. Your mother and I were thrifty over the years, plus my own mother came from a wealthy family in Charleston. I have enough to give you some and still take care of us after the war. You're a smart girl. If you think it's that important, take the gold. Your happiness is worth more to me than any sum of money."

Mariah looked deeply into her pa's face. It was the face of the man she had known before Gettysburg destroyed his pride and self worth. It was the face of the man she had always loved.

Her pa didn't change right away. As she prepared for her trip to Raleigh, he remained grumpy and hard to live with. "Don't know why you had to get mixed up with that spy ring," he would mumble. "You should have a husband, you should be giving grandbabies."

But he gave her the gold, and she noticed that some evenings he would drag the old Bible from the shelf and read for a short time.

"Why did you stop reading the Bible, Pa?" she asked on the night before she left. "You and Ma use to go to church every Sunday and sometimes on Wednesday evenings. You raised me in the church. Why did you stop going?"

"Lost all interest when I got shot up at Gettysburg. Then your ma died. Seemed like God had turned his back on me. The bottle gave me more comfort than the Bible.

"But God's been talking to me. Not in so many words, mind you. That's not the way He operates. But He gave you to me. And for whatever reason, you've stayed with this old man."

In a rare show of emotion, he crossed the room and hugged her. "Be careful up there in Raleigh, girl. If anything happened to you, I would go to the barn and shoot myself."

Mariah knew he was telling the truth.

Early the next morning Mariah hitched up Lucy and headed north. Her students had been delighted when she told them they would have another vacation. Their parents were not. "You're going off again?" Mrs.

Wilson whined. "We may have to find another teacher."

Mariah knew that was unlikely since the male teachers were away fighting and any female who could teach was burdened with her own family. But she decided to placate the woman. "I'll make it up when I get back. I promise to work an extra week in the summer—without pay."

She was blessed to have an extended family in Sampson and Wake Counties. She was an only child but her mother had been one of ten siblings. She knew that her Uncle Rub and Aunt Ellen would welcome her to their farm outside of Clinton.

Uncle Rub saw her as soon as she turned the buggy into his long drive. "You look just like your mother," he said as he helped her to the ground. "I do miss her. How's that no count father of yours?"

"Pa's had a rough time, but he's coming around. You heard that he got shot up at Gettysburg, and then when Ma died...it's been hard on him."

"Come inside. Ellen will set an extra plate. Why in the world are you out by yourself on these dangerous roads? And in the middle of November."

"I'm going to Raleigh. I'll stay with Sally. She doesn't know she's going to have a houseguest, but she is. I had to get away from Brunswick County," Mariah lied. "It's been so depressing living with Pa and with the war and all. With Sally.... you know Sally. There's never a dull minute around her."

"You're telling me. I remember the time you and

that cousin of yours let the mules loose at the family reunion. The boys and I spent the day rounding up those ornery critters instead of visiting with the folks. Why'd you do that, anyway?"

"Seemed like a good idea at the time. We were bored and looking for something to do. Trust me. It was Sally's idea."

That night Mariah luxuriated in the pleasure of being with her aunt and uncle. They had never had children of their own and did their best to spoil her. For one evening she was able to set aside cares and responsibilities and be with people who loved her for no other reason except that she existed.

Uncle Rub helped Mariah hitch Lucy at daybreak. "Why do you have to leave so early, girl? Stay a few days. We would sure enjoy your company."

"Maybe on the way back. Right now I want to get settled with Sally and see what mischief she's up to."

Uncle Rub laughed. "Mischief is the word where Sally's concerned. I don't know why her folks didn't name her Miss Mischief."

Mariah hugged her aunt and uncle and climbed into the buggy. As she flicked the reins, she wondered when she would see them again and what would happen to her before then.

"She ain't here, Miss Mariah," Mary, Sally's old nanny said when Mariah arrived that evening. "But you come in and let me fix you some supper. Don't know when that one will be home, no I don't. She's a wild one and I can't…"

"Who's wild, Mary? And what can't you…Mariah! What are you doing here? How did you manage to drag yourself in from the wilderness to visit us here in civilization?"

Sally had slipped in the back door while Mary was welcoming Mariah at the front of the house. Now she descended on her cousin in a flurry of lace and satin.

As dark as Mariah was, with her straight black hair and olive skin, Sally was the opposite. They were both small, but that was the only resemblance. Sally's blonde curls bobbed in ringlets around her fair, apple polished face. Her huge blue eyes popped with merriment.

"I had to get away, Sal. Pa is impossible and this war has got me so depressed. I knew that wherever you were, something exciting would be happening."

Sally rolled her eyes. "You're right about that— this war is depressing. All the young men are away fighting, or dead, or all shot up. I do my duty, rolling bandages and all. And two days a week I work at the hospital, but I'm tired of being around women and old men.

"You're in luck, though. We're having a card party tonight at the Stevenson's. A Capt. Murray is on special assignment at Camp Magnum. He'll be at the Stevenson's with Major James, the Camp Commander. The Major is engaged to Jane Stevenson so we should have fun. Plus, I'm told this Capt. Murray is easy to look at."

"Shoo," Mary whistled. "You think any male is handsome, Miss Sally. I saw you flirting with old Parson Davis when we went to town yesterday. That man is in his sixties and has a gimpy leg."

Sally rolled her eyes again and led Mariah upstairs. "This is your room," she said. It's right across from mine and we can stay up all night gabbing, if we want. Now, what do you have to wear tonight?"

Mariah looked at the dusty valise that she traveled with. "Nothing, Sally. You know me. I'm a schoolteacher and I live in the country. I only have another brown dress pretty much like the one I'm wearing."

"Well, that will never do. Come to my room and we'll find something. That should be easy since we're the same size."

Mariah knew Sally's family was wealthy, but she didn't realize how little they had been affected by the hardships of the war until she saw Sally's closet. It overflowed with fine dresses, shoes, hats, and shawls. Sally's mother was dead and her father lived abroad. Evidentially he found a way to keep his cherished daughter in style.

"This one, I think," she said, pulling out a bright red satin with black lace sewn on the bodice—"or maybe the green. Do you like green?"

They settled on a modest blue gown with beige trim on the neck and sleeves. "Way too simple," Sally complained. "How are you going to make a play for

Capt. Murray if you look like a schoolmarm?"

"I am a schoolmarm, Sally. This dress will do just fine."

Mariah luxuriated in the bathtub after the housemaid brought up heated water. The maid poured scented oil into the water as her charge soaked her tired muscles. Mariah wished she could stay where she was for hours, but knew Sally was in a hurry. When she stepped out of the tub, she was offered a large towel and imported talcum powder.

Sally burst into the room as her cousin finished dressing. "Are you ready? James has the carriage at the front door."

"Sally," Mariah protested. "I'm starving. We haven't eaten dinner and I've traveled all day."

"No time for that. Besides. I don't eat. I don't want to get fat."

"No chance of that—the way you flutter around. But I do eat and I'm hungry."

"Maybe the Stevenson's will have cake or something. But don't embarrass me by making a pig of yourself." She wrapped a shawl around Mariah and led her from the room.

Mariah followed, her stomach growling in protest.

The Stevenson home was on Oak Street in downtown Raleigh. Mr. Stevenson had been a prosperous merchant before the war and the family lived in a large home, but Mariah noticed that the war had taken its toll on the family wealth as soon as she entered the foyer. The satin curtains were frayed and the wood floor was scuffed. The whole area would have benefitted from a coat of paint.

The war had not dampened the Stevenson's hospitality, however. "Mariah!" Mrs. Stevenson exclaimed when she saw her. "What a treat. Sally didn't tell us that you were visiting."

"I just came this afternoon," Mariah said, leaning forward to be kissed by the older woman. "I surprised Sally. I hope you don't mind that she brought me."

"Mind? We would have been furious if she hadn't. Come into the drawing room. Everyone else is here. And you must meet the handsome Capt. Murray who is here on special assignment."

Mariah went into the next room to greet the assembled group. Mr. Stevenson and Jane rose as she entered. Two military men also stood. She guessed that the major holding Jane's hand was her beau. The other, the one with the knowing smile and in a Confederate officer's uniform, was Capt. Murray, the man she knew to be Jacob McAllister.

"I learned a new card game," Sally exclaimed as soon as the introductions were completed. "It's called Euchre. It's played with a card called the joker. I brought a special deck for us to use."

"I know how to play Euchre," McAllister said.

"You play with partners."

"Then you'll be my partner," Sally insisted. "Since we both know how to play, we can teach the others. Mariah saw Sally favor McAllister with a seductive wink as she sat down.

"Jane, you and Mariah can be partners," Major James told his fiancée. "The rest of us will watch."

"Mariah…" McAllister held out a chair. She sat down and shuddered as his hand softly brushed her neck.

Euchre was a fun and challenging game. Mariah hadn't done anything for pleasure in such a long time that she was soon caught up in the excitement. But her stomach continued to rumble—reminding her that she hadn't eaten since noon.

After four hands, Mariah asked to be excused. The Stevensons were one of the few families she knew to boast indoor plumbing. Mrs. Stevenson showed her to the bathroom and demonstrated how to pull the chain hanging from the ceiling when she was ready to flush.

Mariah could ignore her complaining stomach no longer. After leaving the bathroom, she made her way to the kitchen. She was fortunate that the Stevenson's kitchen was at the back of the house, rather than being a detached structure like most kitchens in large homes.

No one was in the room except for a serving girl. Her eyes widened as Mariah opened cabinets scrounging for something to eat, but she said nothing. Finally, covered by a dishcloth, Mariah found what she was looking for. A baked chicken, browned to perfection, was cooling on the counter.

Her hunger took control as she grabbed a drumstick, ripping it off the bird in eagerness. She sat at the kitchen table and ate greedily.

"Mariah, where are your manners? You're eating like a field hand."

Mariah looked up, grease dripping from her chin. Jacob McAllister was standing in the door mocking her.

"Get out of here, girl," he growled at the kitchen maid who scurried away like a scared rabbit.

"What are you doing here?" she hissed. "Dressed up like a captain in the Confederacy; pretending to be someone you're not. Where did you get that uniform anyway?"

"Let's just say that the man who gave it to me won't ever need it again. Actually, I keep several Confederate uniforms—one for every occasion.

"But I could ask you the same question. What are you doing here? You must have the gold since tomorrow is our deadline."

Mariah glared at him. "I have the gold. It's at Sally's house. I didn't know I'd have to endure spending time with you this evening."

"Mariah, Mariah. Don't talk like that. Ours has been a mutually beneficial relationship. I wouldn't have transacted our business tonight, anyway. Do you think I'd miss the opportunity to take a beautiful woman to lunch? Why maybe after the war you and I could even…"

"Lunch?" Mariah hissed. "There's no way I'm going to lunch with you. Can't we just meet somewhere and transact our business?"

McAllister crossed the room and laid his hand on Mariah's shoulder. "Oh, no my dear, lunch. It's the only way I'll give you the information."

Mariah jerked away and stood up. "I do business with you out of necessity," she growled. "After the war I don't ever want to see you again."

She fled the kitchen, found Sally, and told her they needed to leave.

"You're having lunch with Capt. Murray? At the Carolina Inn?" Sally gushed the next morning. "You must have made quite an impression on him. Can I go, too?"

Mariah looked at Sally through hooded eyes. "I don't think that's what Mc…er, Capt. Murray had in mind. He's sending a carriage at noon."

"Pooh. Then you'll have to tell me all about it when you get back."

McAllister's carriage was on time. When Mariah arrived at the Carolina Inn, he was there to help her down. The wait staff had been well paid to seat them at a choice table. A cozy fire blazed near them warding off the November cold.

"Let's do our business," Mariah demanded. "The

sooner I can leave, the better."

"Oh, no," McAllister laughed. "I have you right where I want you. Now order. Help yourself. You don't have to steal food today like you did last night at the Stevenson's."

"I'm not hungry. Being with you does not whet my appetite."

"Well, I am." McAllister ordered a full meal of roast beef, potatoes, carrots, green beans, and bread. He ordered the same for Mariah. "But first," he told the waiter, "bring us a bottle of your finest Claret. This is a special occasion. Miss Long has agreed to marry me."

"Yes, sir!" the waiter enthused. "Congratulations to both of you."

"Why did you lie?" Mariah hissed as soon as the waiter was out of earshot. "If you were the last man on earth, I wouldn't marry you."

"Maybe you'll change your mind someday. Many women would kill to have that opportunity. But before you claw my eyes out, do you have the gold?"

She opened her purse and showed him her pa's gold. It shone dully in the shadowed room. "What's your information?" she demanded.

The waiter brought the wine and poured them each a glass. After he had left, McAllister proposed a toast. "To us," he said, raising his glass in salute. "To us. Two people who aren't afraid to go after what they want."

"Tell me your information," Mariah repeated. "Let's finish this business so I don't have to look at you anymore."

"My information is that our forces are going to attack the railroad at Willard, North Carolina with all the strength we can muster. It's a small, poorly guarded depot north of Wilmington. In three weeks. We think we should be able to tear up an extensive amount of track and telegraph wires. That's my information. Now give me the gold."

Mariah slid the purse across the table as the waiter set their lunch in front of them. In spite of herself, she ate everything on her plate and even ordered dessert. She had not eaten tender roast beef in many months, and found this meal to be delicious, despite the company.

Chapter 10

"I'se going with you, Mr. Hawk. Ain't nothing you can say make me change my mind. I told you, you'se my kin now that Ma and Pa is dead."

Waddell had made a place for himself in Hawk's unit. Most of the men felt sorry for the young boy who had lost his family in such horrific fashion. "Murdered by our own," they lamented. "He's our responsibility now."

Not all of the soldiers felt that way. One in particular, a small ugly man, Major Percy Pendleton from upstate South Carolina, was the most vocal. "He's a darkie. Why are we taking care of a darkie?"

His sidekick, Larry Simmons, agreed. "Hawk's a darkie lover, that's what."

The two taunted Hawk, calling him "Darkie Man" when they could get away with it.

Those worries were not on Hawk's mind on this day. He was going to leave the boy at camp. "Waddell, you are not going with me. It's dangerous on the road.

You'll stay here with Nance and Jones and Barnes."

"I is going with you. You may be in the Army but I ain't. I don't take orders from nobody. Besides, you need someone to go with you. Who's gonna cook your food and polish your boots?"

"He's right, Hawk." General Hardee overheard the conversation as he approached Hawk's tent. "Frankly, I'm afraid for him to stay here without your protection and I can't babysit him. Pendleton and Larry might see to it that he has an unfortunate 'accident'. Since Pendleton is an officer, though heaven knows how that happened, I can't do much with him. Waddell can go with you and I'm also sending Pvt. Jones."

"Why Jones?" Hawk asked. "Lt. Nance is more experienced. If you're going to send someone, send Nance."

"I need Lt. Nance here, because of his experience. Besides, Pvt. Jones requested to go. I have some dispatches to send with him. He can do that while you're attending to family matters."

"Bet my little sister Brie had something to do with that request," Hawk mumbled as the General left.

The small party left camp the next morning. Hawk had received word that his mother had died of a fever in North Carolina. He had been given leave to go home and bury her.

Waddell swung up onto his pony, anxious for adventure. "Yes sir, I'se got the best little pony in the world. Buttercup, you is as yellow as buttercups in the springtime. You is one beautiful woman."

"Waddell, if you talk all the way to North Carolina, I'm going to tie a rag around your face. Most of the soldiers in the unit think you're special—even gave you that pony—but sometimes, you get on my nerves."

Waddell grinned and was silent for two minutes.

The journey to Tarboro took five days. Their route was littered with burned houses, flattened crops, dead livestock, and destitute citizens.

"This war is destroying the South," Hawk lamented to Pvt. Jones as they skirted yet another destroyed farm. "Sherman and his men have wrecked havoc on these people. I'm told he calls this his 'scorched earth policy.' It's more like the devil in hell was turned loose."

Hawk's sisters Brie and Julia Brown greeted them when they arrived at the Hawkins farm. "We couldn't wait for you," Julia told her brother. "We didn't know when, or if, you'd get here. Mama is buried at Calvary Church. My husband Thomas conducted the service. It was simple, yet beautiful."

"How did she die, Jules? She didn't look sick when I saw her in May."

"She put on a brave front for you while you were here. It was a fever that killed her. Normally she would have been able to shake it off. But she was worn out from trying to keep that farm going and keep body and soul together."

As sad as he was, Hawk was amused by the romance blossoming between Brie and Pvt. Jones. Too shy to speak when anyone else was around, they talked nonstop when they thought no one was listening.

Once Hawk and Julia watched as the couple walked toward the house holding hands. "I believe we'll soon have a new brother-in-law," he told her. "That's all right by me. Pvt. Jones is a fine man. He'll take good care of our little sister."

Hawk, Jones, and Waddell stayed four days in North Carolina. They slept at Julia's house in town so that Hawk, as the oldest surviving son, could attend to legal business regarding the farm.

Early on the morning they were leaving, Julia came into her kitchen to find her brother slumped at the table, his head in his hands. "I know, Hawk," she whispered, putting her hands on his shoulders. "I miss Mama, too. I guess we always will."

"It's not just that, Jules," he sighed. "It's this whole cussed war. I've seen sights no human should be tortured with. We lost Atlanta. You know that. Lt. Gen. Hood made overly aggressive assaults and suffered heavy casualties. I had to try to patch those boys up or hold their hand as they died. I used to write to the families of the boys that died, but now there are just too many. "

"Where is your duty station now?" Julia asked.

"I'm with Gen. William J. Hardee. He requested a transfer from Gen. Hood's army. President Davis made him commander of the Armies of South Carolina, Georgia, and Florida. I think Hood went west.

"Gen. Hardee is a good general but he's fighting a losing battle. We're trying to slow Sherman's march to Savannah, but we don't have enough men or supplies. Sherman calls this his 'March to the Sea' and I'm afraid we can't stop him.

"I don't know how much longer I can last, Jules. Sometimes I want to run away and never look back—maybe go out west."

His sister patted him on the shoulder. There were no words to soothe him. As there was little that was encouraging, she said nothing.

Brie cried as the men left her sister's house. "Take care of yourselves," she shouted as she waved from the front gate. Hawk knew that her tears were as much for Jones as for him.

The road back through North Carolina was not as desolate as that through Georgia. Sherman had yet to turn his wrath northward. Hawk knew it was just a matter of time.

"Get away! Get away from me!" Hawk and his party heard the screaming before they rounded the bend into Castle Hayne, North Carolina.

"Hold up," Hawk commanded. "Let me scout

ahead. We don't want to walk into a trap."

Cautiously, he eased his horse forward, hugging the tree line. What he saw caused him to immediately raise his pistol and fire. Three men were attacking a lone woman. One was holding her horse while the other two were pulling her from the buggy.

The woman was fighting bravely, using her whip to fend off her attackers, but she was no match for them. A red tailed hawk screeched in alarm from a nearby pine.

Hawk's bullet went straight between the eyes of the man holding the woman's horse. He fell backward as the horse reared in fright. The other two men released the woman and groped for their pistols.

A shot rang out behind Hawk. Pvt. Jones had heard the first shot and ridden forward. His bullet killed the ruffian nearest the buggy. The third attacker aimed his gun at Hawk, but fell to the ground before he could shoot. Waddell rode forward brandishing a pistol.

"Where'd you get that, boy? And how'd you learn to shoot like that?" Hawk shouted at him.

"Shooting rabbits for my ma to cook. Got so I never missed. You don't think I'd ride around unarmed, do you? Lt. Nance gave me this pistol 'fore we left. Told me to keep it hidden 'cause you'd be mad. But he said I just might need it. Guess he was right. I saved your hide."

"Hawk!" Jones had ridden to the wagon and grabbed the reins of the terrified horse. "These three men. They're the same ones who killed Waddell's family."

"Well, I'll be," Hawk said after dismounting and examining the bodies. "You're right. Looks like these three decided to make a life out of preying on helpless people instead of going home."

"Gentlemen," the woman in the buggy cried. "I don't know who you are, but I'm certainly glad you came along. I'm not afraid to travel by myself but these three came out of nowhere. Lord knows what would have happened if you hadn't come along."

Hawk looked up at the loveliest face he had ever seen. Long black hair framed a heart-shaped, olive complexioned face. Deep brown eyes, the color of his own, looked down at him. She stretched out a small hand to be helped from the wagon.

"I'm Mariah," she said. "Mariah Long. From Lockwood Folly."

"What in heaven's name are you doing traveling alone on these roads?" Hawk's face was crimson and his eyes blazed. "Have you got no sense woman?"

Mariah bristled. "I had business to attend to. Important business. Besides, I've done this many times and never had a lick of trouble."

Hawk shook his head in disbelief. "Don't you have a husband who would forbid this? Or a father?"

Mariah jutted out her chin. "I'm not married and my father doesn't look after me anymore. His leg was ruined at Gettysburg. He does well to take care of himself."

Hawk struggled to control his anger. "Where are you going? We certainly aren't going to let you go any further by yourself."

"I'm going home. To Lockwood Folly. And I don't need an escort."

"Well, you've got one. Jones, Waddell and I will see you safely delivered to your father."

Mariah and Hawk ignored each other. Pvt. Jones was lost in dreams of Brie Hawkins. Waddell made up for the lack of conversation.

"You sure is pretty, Miss Mariah. Wish you was my schoolmarm. I'd go to school just to look at you. Do you teach colored young'uns?"

Mariah's pa was delighted with the male company when the party arrived at Lockwood Folly. "I get so bored sitting in this cabin staring at the walls. Mariah tries, but there's nothing like talking to a man. Come have a smoke and tell me where you've been. I'll tell you about Gettysburg and how I come to get my leg shot up. How long can you boys stay?"

"Just a few days, Mr. Long. We've already been gone from our unit for over a week. But from the looks of things around here, there are a few chores we could do to leave you and Miss Mariah in better shape. If we can't take care of our own, why are we even fighting this war?"

"Call me Benjamin, please. And you're right. We have things that need fixing that I can't get to and are too much for Mariah."

As pleased as her pa was to have the company, Mariah was in a panic. She had to relay the information McAllister had given her to the Confederates. She hadn't been able to do that in Raleigh for fear of running into him again. And she just couldn't think of a reason to absent herself with all these people underfoot.

Hawk, Jones, and Waddell repaired the roof of the cabin, fixed the back door so that it would shut, and chopped wood for the winter. They also killed a supply of game—deer, rabbits, and squirrels. Hawk taught them how to cut the meat into thin strips and suspend it from racks to dry.

"I wish that we could salt this meat down," he told the others. "That would help preserve it from parasites and make it taste better. But we just don't have the salt. This should keep you through the winter. I've dried meat this way many times when I was hunting."

On the last night of their stay, Mariah and Hawk found themselves alone in the kitchen. Waddell had taught Buttercup to steal hats. Whenever he shouted "Hat!" the horse would sink her teeth into the nearest hat and gallop away. Waddell wanted an audience to watch the trick.

Mariah pleaded that she needed to cook dinner. Hawk seized the opportunity and offered to bring water in for her.

"Miss Mariah..." he began as he hauled the last bucket onto the stove, "I..."

"Don't say anymore, Capt. Hawkins. I need to apologize. I've let my pride take over my manners. You've helped us so much and Pa has thoroughly enjoyed your company. Plus, if the three of you hadn't showed up the other day, I don't know what would have happened. No, I do know what would have happened, and it would have been ugly."

"You're a Confederate spy, aren't you, Mariah?"

Mariah turned toward him, the question obvious on her face. "How did you know?"

"From things you and your pa said, things you thought I wouldn't understand. And you traveling by yourself on that road from Raleigh. You wouldn't have done that unless it was a dire situation. Tell me what you learned. Let me help."

Feeling the weight drop from her shoulders, she slumped in a chair and covered her face with her hands. Then she told him—about Jacob McAllister, about the planned attack on the railroad at Willard, and about her need to relay that information to the Confederates.

"I can do that for you," Hawk said. "That will be no problem. We'll take a little detour to Wilmington tomorrow and telegraph the news to our forces who can intercept the Yankees. We're a little pushed for time, but it will work."

They heard the others walking toward the house. Hawk knew he wouldn't have another opportunity to say what was on his mind. "You're a brave woman, Mariah. The bravest I've ever met. Also the most beautiful. Could I write to you after I get back to my duty station? Would you answer my letters? And will you call me Hawk?"

Mariah looked up at him through thick, moist eyelashes. "I would answer your letters, Hawk...with pleasure," she whispered.

Chapter 11

Hawk and his party delivered Mariah's information to the officers at Ft. Fisher, just outside of Wilmington.

"Can you boys hold off the Yankees?" Hawk asked the commanding officer.

"We don't have any choice. We must keep the port of Wilmington opened so that supplies can get to Lee's army. We have sandbags and earthen works, but I could sure use some reinforcements."

The Commander told Hawk that Hardee's soldiers were heading toward Savannah, Georgia. "That's where Sherman is going. For a while we thought it might be Macon, but that old fox is making his way to Ft. Pulaski and the port of Savannah. He may get there by Christmas. He's destroying everything in his path."

As they made their way through Georgia, Hawk's party saw more evidence of Sherman's destruction. "Did you see trees with metal wrapped around them?" a farmer asked when they stopped for water. "We call those 'Sherman's neckties'. They tear up our railroad tracks and twist them around the trees.

"Sherman's not worried about supplies. I heard he gave orders for his men to live off the land. And that's what they're doing."

Hawk and his men were appalled by the devastation—homes and barns burned, livestock slaughtered, crops and fields laid waste. "Why do they destroy everything?" he asked the others. "These people are simple farmers. They don't own slaves."

As they rounded a bend, they saw more destruction. A small farm, the house standing but the barns and crops burned, stood at the end of the road. As they drew closer, they heard uncontrolled sobbing.

"Why'd they kill you, Bobo?" a little girl wailed. She sat in the dirt, clutching a scraggly dead puppy. "You didn't do anything, Bobo. You barked a little, but that was because you were scared. Why'd they have to kill you?"

Behind her a man, likely her father, cried with her. He looked up when he saw Hawk and his men. "That puppy was all she had to give her comfort," he told them. "Her mother, my wife, died of the fever in May. That puppy kept my little girl alive. He lay beside her and licked her face while she was sick. She got well so she could be with him."

Somewhere, deep in his soul, Hawk sensed a door slam shut and a key turn. He knew he had crossed the threshold of believing that there were redeeming qualities to this war.

The men let the little girl mourn, then Waddell got off Buttercup and walked to her. "Tell me about Bobo," he whispered. "Then I'll help you bury him. We'll find a nice spot where you can talk to him everyday. He'll be with you, even though you can't see him. That's what I do with my folks. They're in heaven, now. They'll take care of Bobo."

Hawk realized then that he loved the kind hearted boy. Waddell had come into his life through tragedy, but it was true. They were kin now.

Hawk, Jones, and Waddell met Lt. Gen. Hardee and his troops outside of Savannah on the first day of December 1864. The day was cold and miserable; the soldiers disheartened.

"We're doing what we can to slow Sherman," Hardee told them. "But it's useless. We're outnumbered and outgunned. It's a matter of time before they take Savannah, unless there's a miracle. And I don't see that happening. All we can do is try to slow their advance."

Life for the soldiers settled into a predictable routine. Barnes, Jones, and Nance had their duties. Hawk patched up wounds, lanced boils, treated dysentery, and pulled teeth. Waddell was bored.

"Let's go hunting this afternoon," he begged Hawk. "We could snag a rabbit or two. Fresh meat would be right tasty for dinner tonight."

"I can't go, Waddell. I've got duties. You stay out of trouble and I'll see you at dinner."

Waddell fumed. He tried to occupy his time, but could not. Finally, he went to see Buttercup. "I can't take you, girl," he told his pony. "Soon as Hawk sees you're gone, he'll come looking for me. Then he'll tan my hide. I'll slip away and be back 'fore anyone knows I'm gone. And we'll have fresh rabbit or squirrel for dinner."

Pendleton and Larry watched as the boy slipped into the woods, rifle in hand. "Now's our chance," Pendleton told his lackey. "We'll teach that black boy a lesson he'll never forget." And they followed.

The boy hadn't gone far before the men overtook him. Each grabbed an arm and manhandled him to the nearest tree. As they tied him, Waddell protested.

"What is I ever done to you?" he demanded. "I polished your boots and cooked your meals. Why is you bothering me?"

"Cause you're black," Pendleton hissed as he cinched the rope tightly. "And we don't like black people. They smell bad and have lice."

"I may be black," Waddell shouted, "but I ain't ugly. You two is 'bout the ugliest human beings I ever seed."

Pendleton slapped the boy across the face. "We're going to teach you some manners, darkie. We're going to teach you to respect your elders—specially if they're white."

For the next half hour, Pendleton and Larry burned the boy with cigarettes, urinated on him, and spit in his face. Then they grew bored.

"Shall we kill him?" Larry asked. "Let's kill him and see if black people die like white people do."

"Nah, I don't want to go to jail for the likes of this darkie. Leave him here. Hawk will find him after while, but we'll be long gone."

At sundown, Hawk began to wonder why he hadn't seen Waddell all afternoon. By dark, he became worried. Buttercup was tethered with the other horses, so he must have left on foot. Taking a lantern, he began to track the boy into the woods.

When Hawk found Waddell he was still tied to the tree. The child was semiconscious. "Who did this to you?" Hawk demanded, although he knew the answer.

"P-p-pendton," Waddell rasped through parched lips. "P-pendleton and Larry."

Hawk untied the boy and cradled him in his arms. "Sh-h," he murmured. "Let me get you back to camp so I can tend to you."

By lamplight, Hawk and Jones washed the child and treated his wounds. Hawk called Gen. Hardee to the medical tent. Waddell was sleeping, but the damage was evident.

"He said Pendleton and Larry did this," Hawk told his commander.

"I'll find them. There's no excuse for abusing a child and I won't have it in my unit."

Hardee returned with his face twisted into a scowl. "Pendleton says he's been here all afternoon. Larry vouches for him. No one else will speak up. His men are scared. Just don't let that boy out of your sight. You, Barnes, Jones, or Nance should be with him all the time."

Waddell was young. He healed quickly. Hawk was amazed that the child's sunny disposition remained intact. "My daddy told me most people is good. But some ain't. Some's got the devil in them. That's Pendleton and Larry for sure."

From then on, Waddell stayed close to Hawk and his men. If he saw Pendleton or Larry he would shudder and run for cover. Their leering smiles were proof that they had harmed the boy, but Hawk could find no way to retaliate.

As December moved toward Christmas, Hardee's men retreated closer and closer toward Savannah. The mood of the unit was desolate. They were waiting for the inevitable.

To Hawk, the one bright spot were the letters he was receiving from Mariah. She wrote often. Sometimes he would get three letters at a time. Other times he would go a week or more without hearing from her.

Hawk knew that he had never felt this way about a woman before. He'd never desired any female with such passion. This tiny scrap of a woman had wheedled her way into his heart. This gave him cause to smile when nothing else did. Perhaps he was being foolish, but he didn't care.

Mariah wrote of life with her father, of the antics of her school children, of her work with the churchwomen as they gathered supplies and made clothing for the soldiers. She never mentioned her work as a spy. Hawk assumed that was a thing of the past. At this point, any knowledge was almost useless.

Hawk wrote just as frequently. He didn't tell her about Waddell's injuries, and couldn't say where his unit was stationed, but there was enough going on at camp to make his letters interesting. He said he missed her and couldn't wait to spend time with her.

Gradually their letters were turning toward the future—their future.

Chapter 12

"Mariah, you've got another letter from that boy." Benjamin Long was secretly pleased that Mariah and the handsome Confederate were corresponding. His wayward daughter needed a man in her life. "Jeb picked it up in town and just now dropped it off."

Mariah rushed to her father and grabbed the letter. Tearing it from his hand, she ran outside. She didn't want her pa to see her blush if this letter followed the same vein that Hawk's letters had begun to take.

"So, what did he have to say?" Benjamin asked when she returned to the kitchen.

"Oh, nothing much. They're low on supplies—things that churchwomen can make. I'm going to the church this afternoon to work. We can mend old socks, maybe even find material for new ones. And we can repair our husband's and father's worn out clothes for the soldiers. I'm working on your plaid shirt right now."

"That's my favorite shirt. Take the red one."

"The plaid one is in the best condition. Some

soldier needs it worse than you do."

"How about that crop of apples? Are you doing anything with them?"

"I've put them out to dry and Pa..."

"Uh, oh. What does 'and Pa' mean?"

"I'm going to have to deliver these goods to the troops at some point. They aren't doing the soldiers any good if they're stored at the church. And one more thing..."

"Oh, Lord. What's 'and one more thing?'"

"Actually, that's it. The Lord has a lot to do with it. Could we go to Christmas services at church?"

"We can, Mariah. I'd like that."

Mariah and her pa were greeted warmly that Christmas Day. Their neighbors told Pa that they had missed seeing him and they thought he was brave. Pastor James sermon was boring. How do you put your parishioners to sleep with the Christmas message? Pastor James found a way.

Something happened at the end of the service that woke them up, though. Tommy Tyler, the telegraph operator, burst through the church doors. "Savannah has fallen," he shouted, "on December 22. Gen. Hardee escaped with 10,000 men, and Sherman moved in. Told Lincoln he was presenting him with the city of Savannah as a Christmas gift."

Mariah clutched her pa's arm. Although she didn't know exactly where Hawk was, he was with

Gen. Hardee. She prayed that he had escaped with the General.

The following week Mariah received a letter. Hawk was safe and he was coming to see her. He had told the General about the supplies the churchwomen had collected. The General had told him to come.

"He wants me to thank the women personally," Hawk's letter said. "And there's not much I can do around here. We're retreating. I won't be needed until we fight again—and we will. Besides, I think the General knows about us."

Mariah was overjoyed. She insisted that her pa clean himself up and help her straighten the house. "Dangit, woman," he complained. "Hawk's a soldier. He doesn't care if I'm clean-shaven or not."

"We don't know what day he'll arrive. I want us to be ready."

Hawk arrived within the week. Waddell was with him. They brought two packhorses for the supplies.

The first night they were there, he told Mariah about the abuse Waddell had received at the hands of their own soldiers. "I've never wanted to kill Yankees as badly as I'd like to kill those two," he growled. "It doesn't seem to have affected Waddell. That boy has been through hell. I don't see how he stays so happy.

"Can I thank the churchwomen?" Hawk asked. "Maybe that would be encouragement for them—to have a soldier tell them how important their work is to those of us on the front."

"We have a meeting tomorrow morning," Mariah told him. "Come with me."

The next day, Hawk faced a group of wives, mothers, sisters and sweethearts. All were anxious to hear details of the fighting and to ask if Hawk knew their loved one.

"Sometimes, when I'm patching up boys who aren't old enough to shave, I don't believe in God," he told the women. "But I do believe that you ladies are doing God's work, if there is a God. Thank you. Thank you from all the soldiers and please don't stop your efforts."

Too soon it was time for Hawk to leave. "Hardee needs these supplies," he said. "We're low on everything. The clothing and food will be most welcome."

They were sitting on the front porch holding hands in the dark. Hawk leaned over and kissed her. It wasn't their first kiss, but was made especially sweet because it would be their last. For some time anyway.

Chapter 13

"Gen. Grant is coming to inspect our troops! All soldiers who have won medals will be at the front of the receiving line, wearing their medals. Spit and polish! Capt. McAllister, since you've won the Medal of Honor and are newly promoted, you'll be first in line." Gen. Wessells could hardly contain his excitement as he addressed his officers.

"Uh, General, I need to speak to you in private," McAllister whispered as soon as he could get Wessell's attention.

"What is it, Captain? Aren't you pleased with this honor?" Wessells questioned when they were alone in his tent.

"I am, sir. I am. It's just that, well, ah, I don't have the medal in my possession."

"You what? You don't have your Medal of Honor?"

"No sir. I, ah, well, ah, I lost it."

"You lost it! How could you lose the Medal of Honor?"

"I haven't seen it since the Battle of Plymouth," he lied, remembering that the last time he'd had the medal in his possession was the day he'd raped Betsy Brody. "Foolishly, I wore it into battle—thinking it might scare a few Rebels. It was torn from my shirt in the heat of fighting. Probably some Johnny Reb is wearing it now."

"You idiot!" Wessells shouted. "How could you do something so stupid? You're an excellent scout, McAllister, but sometimes I question your judgment."

McAllister hung his head. There was nothing he could say.

"Grant knows we have a Medal of Honor winner among us. He'll be looking for you. What in heaven's name will I tell him?"

Again, McAllister had no answer.

"You can't be here. I'll tell Grant that I had to send my finest officer on an important mission. He'll believe that. And what will that mission be? There's nothing that needs doing except herding a passel of mules to replenish the troops in Raleigh. You're so fond of animals. That's your important mission. And those mules better be in tip-top shape when you deliver them."

Secretly, McAllister was pleased to get off so lightly. He'd envisioned court martial or something equally sinister. He had a motive for wanting to return to Raleigh—Mariah Long's cousin Sally.

Sally didn't interest him, although she was vivacious and pretty. It was Mariah who tantalized. He admired her spunk and courage, not to mention her beauty. Sally could tell him how to find Mariah.

Before he rounded up his mules, he packed his Confederate uniform. The uniform of Captain Alonzo Murray, Confederate States of America was pressed back into service.

Herding the mules to Raleigh was a thankless task. McAllister thought it might have been easier to face Gen. Grant. Wessells had chosen a fitting punishment for him.

He had two privates to help, but Wessells had given him the twenty most ornery mules in the Union Army. That made sense, though. The General would have wanted to weed out the troublemakers.

"Get that stupid mule back with the group," he yelled for the fiftieth time that day. A large, mean-spirited animal had decided to wander off the road and eat sunflowers. "I do love animals," he grumbled to himself, "but I'm not sure mules are animals. They're devils in disguise."

Finally he delivered his charges. "Gen. Wessell sends his finest," he told the mule boss, smirking at the privates. The Raleigh soldiers would find out soon enough.

"You fellows entertain yourselves this evening," he told his men. "I know a certain lonely lady who thinks I'm a dashing Confederate Captain. I'll see you in the morning."

"Why Capt. Murray!" Sally answered the door herself and was thrilled to see McAllister.

"What a pleasant surprise. I thought you were smitten with my cousin Mariah. Are you in town for long?"

"Please. Call me Alonzo. And no, I have leave for this evening only. Then I must report back to Camp Magnum. The war is not going as we would wish, but you're a pretty diversion."

"Then we'll make good use of the evening. Have you eaten?"

Mary served them a sparse meal of root vegetables and cornbread. McAllister noted that his soldier's rations were more plentiful than Sally's.

She sensed his displeasure. "I'm afraid that's all we have. And we're lucky to have this. Mary was sensible and had a garden this fall. It's been a long time since we've eaten meat."

"The pleasure is being with you, Miss Sally," he countered. "Let's not speak of war tonight. Not at all. Let's talk of life after the fighting ends."

Sally told him of the trouble she and Mariah managed to get into whenever they were together. He lied about the exploits of the fictitious Confederate Capt. Murray.

"Did you hear about how we thwarted the Yankees when they tried to tear up the railroad tracks at Willard?" he asked, remembering that he had supplied Mariah with information about the raid. "I led that attack."

By ten o'clock, Mary's hints for him to leave were becoming blatant. He had learned what he wanted to know. Mariah lived with her father Benjamin on the Lockwood Folly River in Brunswick County. She should be easy to find.

Sally walked with him onto the porch. McAllister saw Mary peaking through the curtains, observing her charge. As he tipped his hat in thanks for a lovely evening, Sally reached up and kissed him on the lips.

"Come back, safely, Alonzo," she whispered. "I'll be here waiting for you."

As soon as she went back in the house, he heard Mary's fussing. "Have you got no pride or shame, girl? Kissing a man the first time he comes to call?"

McAllister smiled into the darkness. Two cousins— both extraordinary. Maybe he wouldn't have to choose.

Chapter 14

Mariah knew from Hawk's letters that Hardee's forces were retreating from Savannah. The churchwomen continued gathering supplies for the men.

In late December, they rejoiced to hear that the Union forces had been defeated when they attacked Ft. Fisher. By mid January 1865, they mourned the loss of the fort.

"It's a matter of time," Hawk wrote. "Ft. Fisher guarded our last open port. All we can do now is retreat."

From January to March, Hardee retreated northward, hoping to unite with Gen. Lee and other Confederate forces.

Mariah continued writing to Hawk. That gave her some measure of purpose. "I have more supplies," she wrote. "Where can I meet you?"

Hawk could give no definitive answer. He didn't know himself. "North," was all he could say. "We're going north."

"Then I'm going north," Mariah told her pa. "I'll ask everyone wearing a Confederate uniform if they know the whereabouts of Gen. Hardee. Someone must have some information."

"You're foolish, girl," Benjamin answered. "A woman alone on these roads? I'm going with you. I've hidden in this house long enough."

Nothing she could say would discourage him, and in a way, Mariah was glad. Her pa was much stronger than he had been and he'd always been a crack shot with a rifle.

One bright morning in early March the pair loaded the supplies in their buckboard and hitched up Lucy. "We'll stay with friends and family as much as possible," Mariah told her father. "But we may have to camp out some nights. Are you up for that?"

The look her pa gave her was comical. "Girl," he snarled. "I was camping out before you were born. These bones may creak, but they still work."

They spent the first night with Aunt Tillie in Wilmington. That was a true measure of Mariah's father's resolve to be useful.

"Benjamin," Tillie fussed. "You're too old to set off on this hair-brained adventure of Mariah's. And she has no business going off by herself. You two stay here until this war is over—which won't be much longer, I assure you."

"I'd rather be captured by the Yankees," Benjamin grumbled.

The stop at Aunt Tillie's turned out to be a good thing. Tillie and her friends had been stockpiling supplies and were thrilled to have an avenue to send them to the front. They added their goods to the Longs'.

The locals also had information about Hardee and his troops. "They passed nearby," a neighbor said. "They couldn't tell us where they were going, but hinted they were headed toward the middle of the state—maybe Goldsboro or Fayetteville."

The next morning, Mariah and Benjamin set out toward Goldsboro.

They traveled all day. By dark Mariah, Benjamin, even Lucy, were exhausted. They were miles from anyone they knew, so decided to camp. Pa pitched their small tent and fed Lucy while Mariah made a fire and fixed a meager supper of beans and cornbread.

Father and daughter sat by the fire long after they had finished their meal. "Sure is quiet out here," Benjamin observed. "Quiet and dark. There must be a billion stars in the sky."

"Do you ever think about Ma?" Mariah asked.

Her pa wiped his eyes. "All the time. Like tonight. One of those stars is your ma looking down on us and watching over us. I think I'll be with her soon."

"Pa! Don't say that. I need you here with me."

"No you don't, girl. Soon's this war's over you'll hook up with Hawk, and that's a good thing. You're strong. You'll make a good life for yourself. You two will make beautiful babies. I'm ready. I'm ready to be with your ma."

Sadness overwhelmed Mariah. She couldn't imagine life without her pa, but it might come to that.

The next morning Mariah was stiff in every part of her body. The ground had been cold and hard. Her pa was grumpy. Only Lucy was ready for the day ahead. She had rested and munched on new spring grass. She tossed her head when Mariah tried to harness her.

"Come on girl, settle down," Mariah murmured to the frisky horse. "We've got a full day ahead. I don't know where we'll sleep tonight."

"Hardee?" a farmer asked. "He was through here two days ago. He was headed toward Bentonville."

They headed toward Bentonville.

"It's March 16, 1865," Benjamin reminded Mariah. "Do you know what day this is?"

"Nothing special. Is it the first day of spring?"

"It's your birthday, girl! You were born twenty two years ago today. Your ma and I thought you were the prettiest little thing we ever saw. You were so small and your ma had a hard time birthing you. Bet you didn't weigh mor'n than four pounds."

"Is that why you never had any more children?"

"It is. I had you and your ma. What else did I need?"

Mariah reached for her pa's hand. He had gone through rough times, but was coming back to life.

By nightfall, they overtook the soldiers. "Better stay away, folks," they were told. "Sherman's up ahead.

This is likely to be the final showdown."

"Do you know where Gen. Hardee's men are?" Mariah asked. "Do you know a surgeon named Hawkins? He has a little black boy traveling with him."

"You mean Waddell? Ain't that young'un something? He can make you laugh on the worse day of your life. Hawk sure does love that boy. They're ahead of us—the next column up. But you should turn around and go home."

"Let's camp here tonight," Mariah suggested. "We'd never find Hawk in this darkness."

Hawk was not pleased to see them. "We need the supplies, Mariah," he grumbled. "But you've put yourself and your pa in danger. Of course, I'm glad to see you, but you're a liability. I can't protect you and take care of these men too."

It was then that Mariah realized that what Hawk said was true. She had been so intent on seeing him and delivering the supplies she hadn't stopped to think of the position she'd put him in.

"We'll leave tomorrow. I'm sorry. I didn't think."

He leaned down and kissed her—in front of her pa and the soldiers. "I'm glad you didn't," he whispered.

Mariah could barely hear him over the catcalls and whistles.

March 18th dawned as miserable as the days before. Mariah and Benjamin unloaded their wagon and made ready to leave. Mariah hadn't seen Hawk since the night before.

Then he was there—shouting and gesturing wildly. "Move to the left," he shouted. "Johnston has decided to wage a surprise attack on Sherman's troops. Go left, away from the fighting, then get out of here as fast as you can."

They did what he said. Mariah touched Lucy with the whip and she broke into a gallop. Soon they were away from the fighting and Mariah slowed her horse to a trot. They seemed safe.

"What's that?" Benjamin shouted. "In front of us."

"The Yankees have swung left, Pa. Our boys have turned them, but they're heading in our direction."

Soon they were upon the Longs. A blue-coated soldier grabbed Lucy's reins and another pulled Mariah from the wagon.

"Well, my pretty," he chuckled. "The spoils of war."

Benjamin used the whip in an attempt to fend off the soldiers, but it did no good. Then he reached under his seat and pulled out his shotgun.

"Leave my girl alone!" he shouted as he shot Mariah's captor through the head.

The soldier holding Lucy reached for his pistol and aimed it at Benjamin. Mariah heard the shot, then blacked out and knew no more.

When she came to, Hawk was bathing her face with water. "Pa?" she asked.

"Your pa is dead, Mariah. He died protecting you. We came over the hill and chased the Yankees away.

But it was too late to save your pa."

Mariah sagged against Hawk, fighting the darkness that again reached for her. "Pa? Pa's dead? That can't be. Not my Pa."

Hawk didn't answer. He just held Mariah and rocked her gently. Eventually, he felt her body stiffen and she rose up and squared her shoulders.

"Where is he now?" she whispered.

"In the buckboard. You have kin in Raleigh, don't you?"

"My cousin Sally. I can take Pa there and bury him."

"Waddell is going with you. He's a good shot and I want him out of this fighting. You two need each other now."

"Sally lives on Oak Street. Everyone knows her. Come as soon as you can."

"As soon as I can." Hawk caressed her face. "When I get there, I want you to marry me. We'll find a preacher somewhere."

The sad little group left the battlefield, heading toward Raleigh to bury the man who had loved his daughter since the day she was born. "I've never been so sad," she whispered to no one in particular. "So sad and yet so happy."

Chapter 15

The advancements at Bentonville were short lived. Reinforcements swelled Sherman's troops. Bloody fighting forced the Confederates to retreat, Hardee's troops among them.

"I can't find Jones," Hawk shouted to Nance. "Have you seen him?"

"Last I knew he was pursuing a Yankee into the midst of the fighting. He's a brash young kid. He may have gotten himself kilt."

"My sister Brie would never forgive me if I let that happen. I better find him."

Undercover of nightfall, Hawk retraced the retreat. Around him he heard moans and cries for help from the wounded—on both sides. The blood and gore sickened him.

"Jones," he called softly. "Where in the name of all that's holy are you?"

"Here," he finally heard from a heap that had fallen in a grotesque pile of mud and rags.

Squatting on the ground, he searched for the boy's face.

"What have you done you stupid fool?" he growled. "Brie will kill me." Turning Jones on his side, Hawk saw an open gash that slashed across his abdomen. The soldier was holding his intestines to his body with his free hand.

"I'm not going to live, am I Hawk?" Jones cried softly. "I want a life. I want to marry your sister."

"You'll live if I have anything to do with it. Sorry as you are, you're destined to be my brother-in-law.

"I have to pick you up. It will hurt, but I've got to get you back so I can examine you."

Hawk picked the boy up like a baby, trying to staunch the loss of blood and fluid. Treading carefully, he stepped over corpses and the wounded. Once, holding Jones close to his chest, he stopped to vomit at the sight of a soldier's brains spread across his smashed face.

"I can't take it anymore," he whispered into the night. "I've seen too much. This war is over for me."

Jones had lost consciousness. Hawk laid him on the operating table and called for lanterns. He and Nance worked late into the night, wiping his forehead, washing his wounds, and sewing up his chest.

"It's up to God now," Hawk said as the sun rose in the east. "We'll have to move him soon, and that's not what he needs."

Jones was young and in love. In spite of the odds, he began to improve. In three days he could sit up and swallow soup. At the end of the week, he could sit on a horse.

By then, Hardee's men had retreated to Raleigh. Hawk approached his commander for a medical discharge for Jones. "He's no use to us," Hawk reasoned. "He's a liability and takes up too much of my time. Let me put him on his horse and send him to my sister. That's the best medicine for him now."

One bright sunny morning in the first week of April, Jones left for Tarboro. "If your side starts bleeding, stop and change the bandages. Brie will take care of you when you get to Julia's house."

"Why do I feel lucky?" Jones laughed. "Here I've got a terrible wound and that wound is sending me to the woman I love."

"Just behave yourself until I get there," Hawk cautioned.

Chapter 16

Sally was not pleased that her cousin and a young boy would be with her—probably until the end of the war.

"She need somebody to keep up with her," Mary fumed. "Lord knows I can't. That Capt. Murray spends more time with us than with his men."

"Is that why Sally is being so cold to me, Mary? Is she afraid I'll steal her beau?"

"Lord knows, Ma'am. Youse welcome to take him if'n you wants him."

"No thank you. Not that one. Sally can have him. Besides, I've got a man of my own. We're getting married as soon as his unit gets to Raleigh."

Before Mary could ask questions, Mariah turned on her heel and went to look for Sally.

McAllister came frequently. He and Mariah acknowledged each other, but it was Sally who held his attention. She relaxed when she realized that Mariah was no threat and accepted the fact that her guests were with her for the duration of the war.

McAllister was sly. When Sally wasn't around he shot suggestive looks or raised his eyebrows at Mariah. Once he asked her to meet him at the Carolina Inn for another lunch date. She ignored him.

Mariah didn't see Hawk for three weeks. And then he was there. He came one evening as they were finishing their dinner.

"I only have a few hours," he whispered when he and Mariah assumed they were alone. "I wish we could find a preacher to marry us. I'd sure like to spend tonight with you."

Waddell, who seemed to be everywhere and know everything, spoke up. "I can marry you. I told you I was my dad's 'sistant preacher. I'se done lots of weddings."

"Thanks, Waddell," Hawk chuckled. "But we want our marriage to be legal."

"This'll be legal. You can go down to the courthouse tomorrow, pay the man, and get a 'ficial certificate. My name bes in their books. Waddell Waddell—assistant pastor, Waddell AME Church.

So the strange wedding party assembled in Sally's parlor. Sally played a wedding march on the family grand piano. Mary was Mariah's matron of honor. Waddell stood before the fireplace holding an old prayer book.

"Hawk," he began, lowering his voice to control

the pitch changes that had started appearing in his speech. "Do you take this woman to have and to hold—forever?"

"I do," Hawk whispered. "Forever and ever."

"Mariah, will you do the same for Hawk?"

Mariah looked into Hawk's eyes. She knew she would never regret her next words. "Forever and ever."

"Then by the power gived me by the state of North Carolina, you two is man and wife together."

Sally and Mary had outdone themselves. In the hour's notice she'd been given that a wedding was to take place, Mary had put together a respectable meal. She had found a ham and jelly for biscuits and then opened a bottle of sherry.

Neither Hawk or Mariah were hungry, so they begged off as soon as was polite. Waddell, though, was enjoying his first taste of spirits.

Sally had turned the master bedroom into her version of what a wedding suite should look like. She had taken white satin and gauze from an old ball gown and had draped it over the bed and all the furniture.

"I feel like I'm going to a funeral rather than my wedding night," Hawk grumbled. He tore the gauze off the bedposts and threw it on the floor. Then his thoughts turned to other matters.

"Mariah," he growled in deep guttural tones that were part emotion but mostly raw passion. "I never thought this night would come. I hope what Waddell says it true and that this is legal, but right now, I really don't care."

They spent the night in each other's arms—sometimes sleeping, sometimes whispering love words, and sometimes giving in to the splendor of marital pleasures.

Too soon it was morning.

"I have to go," Hawk whispered. "I only had last night. I'll come back as soon as I can and we'll go to the courthouse to be certain we're legally married."

"I'se going with you," Waddell declared when Hawk came down the front steps. Buttercup was saddled and carrying all of Waddell's worldly belongings.

"I'se tired of being here with a passel of women. All I hear is 'Is you washed your face? Is you studied your lesson? Go fetch me some wood for the fire.' You'se got to take me out of here."

"Waddell, you can't..." Mariah began.

"It's all right." Hawk gave the boy a leg up on Buttercup. "The fighting's over. He won't be in danger now."

Hawk went to get his horse, and then came back for one last kiss. "Good-bye, Mariah Hawkins." He beamed a sunny smile, but his eyes reflected Mariah's own tears.

The next morning Mariah went to the state capital.

"Yes, Ma'am," the clerk announced after pouring over a gigantic ledger. "Here it is, Waddell AME Church, Waddell, North Carolina. Pastor James

Waddell, assistant pastor Waddell Waddell. If this Rev. Waddell Waddell married you, then I'd say it's legal. That'll be two dollars, please, and you'll need to fill out some paperwork."

Mariah snickered. Rev. Waddell Waddell? But she was relieved. After the love Hawk and I shared last night, I want to be right with God and the law, she thought. "I'll be back as soon as I can get signatures from the preacher and the witnesses," she told the clerk. "Here is the two dollars if you would please go ahead and enter our names."

Chapter 17

Life for Hawk and the rest of the Confederates became a test of nerves. They knew surrender was near, but were apprehensive about their fate. Would they be tried as criminals? Would they be allowed to go free? And they were bored. They were not used to being in camp with nowhere to go and no one to fight.

Pendleton and Larry were the worse. With no target for their hostilities, they turned to Waddell.

Often, as he walked by an isolated building or tent, Larry would jump out shouting "Boo!" and making grotesque faces.

At mealtime or when he was trying to fall asleep, he'd hear the catcalls, "Wad—dell, Wad—dellie. What 'cha doing black boy? Boogie Man gonna get you."

His tent was vandalized and his clothes scattered.

The two preyed on Buttercup as well, tying her mane in knots and spreading mud and manure on her coat. Pendleton's horse was a biter. Waddell would often find Buttercup tethered next to the beast, teeth marks on her flanks and withers.

Waddell complained to Hawk but got no help. "Try to stay out of their way, boy. Soon enough we'll be done with those two."

April 11, 1865 was a mild, early spring day in Raleigh. Some of the battle weary Confederates took no notice of the balmy weather. Others responded with unabashed spring fever. Waddell was one of those.

"We'se going to get Pendleton and Larry today," he whispered to Buttercup as he brushed the most recent knots out of her mane. "I don't know how, but I'se had it. And that no good Hawk won't do nothing."

Rumors flew among the soldiers, enhanced as they traveled from man to man. "We're all going to be hanged by the end of the week," was the latest. "But first we're going to be drawn and quartered—officers first."

Hawk and Lance sat near their tents, trying to ignore what they heard. Men always made up their own version of the truth when they were uncertain of the future. Often it was far worse than reality.

Shouting on the road into the camp demanded their attention. "The Yankees are running loose in Raleigh," a soldier hollered as he rode in on a sweat soaked horse. "They're on Oak Street, raping women and making them walk naked in the street. I saw it with my own eyes."

"Oak Street," Hawk shouted, jumping to his feet.. "That's where Sally lives—and Mariah is with her. I've got to go there."

Lance grabbed his arm. "You can't just leave, Hawk. You'll be called a deserter. Remember Governor Vance ordered all deserters to be hung."

"I can't just stay here," Hawk fumed. "I'm at least going to the end of road to see what I can see."

The other soldiers had the same idea, their curiosity fueled by the shouting horseman—Pendleton and Larry included.

"Now's our chance," Waddell told Buttercup. "We'll make them the laughingstock of the whole company.

He patted the pony and swung onto her back. Easing around the mob of soldiers so they wouldn't be seen, he maneuvered to within an arm's length of his two enemies.

At the top of his lungs Waddell shouted, "Hat!"

Buttercup stretched her neck out and grabbed Pendleton's pride and joy—his grey felt hat, complete with feather, proving that he was a major in the Confederate army.

Tossing her head, Buttercup clenched the hat in her teeth and galloped off.

"What the...?" the surprised Pendleton shouted. "Larry, get that little..."

Before Pendleton finished his sentence, Larry

drew his pistol and shot Waddell in the back. The boy tumbled from the fleeing horse and lay face down in the dirt.

Hawk watched in horror as the scene unfolded. He and Lance rushed to the boy as the other soldiers hurried out of their way. Cradling Waddell's head, Hawk checked for signs of life.

"He's not breathing, Lance," he cried. "Waddell's dead! He's not breathing!"

As he rested his head on Waddell's chest another rider entered camp. "Now the Yankees are murdering civilians in Raleigh," the soldier shouted. "Say they'll murder and burn, just like they did in Atlanta."

Hawk looked up at Lance. "Bury him," he instructed. "Take Waddell back to my home in Tarboro and bury him. I'm going to find Mariah."

Chapter 18

McAllister, dressed as Capt. Murray, smiled to himself as he trotted down the road to Sally's house. The war was almost over and he had a nice stash of Confederate gold in the bank. Sally was in love with him but he hadn't decided. Who would it be—Sally or Mariah? Mariah couldn't seem to get her mind off that guy named Hawk. Hawk…what a stupid name…a bird name…. He drew his horse up short.

"What in the name of all that's holy do you think you're doing?" McAllister jumped to the ground and grabbed the arm of the man who was brutally whipping a little yellow horse.

The horse had a tattered grey hat sporting a wilted feather clenched in its teeth.

"That dang horse got my hat," Pendleton growled. "I'm going to teach her a lesson she'll never forget."

"Lay one more blow on her and it'll be the last thing you ever do." McAllister drew his pistol, the ire he felt whenever an animal was mistreated rose in his throat.

"That's Buttercup—Waddell's horse," McAllister lowered his pistol and stared at the pony. The fight had gone out of Pendleton, the whip hanging limp by his side.

"What are you doing with Buttercup, and where's Waddell?"

"Gone to meet his maker, I hope. My partner Larry took care of that with his gun."

"You're beating this horse? Over a stupid hat?" McAllister shook his head in disbelief. "And you shot Waddell?" he added as an afterthought.

"Larry shot him, I'm innocent."

"I'll bet. Get out of the way. I'll take Buttercup to Sally's and find out what's going on."

The Confederates surrounded Larry. "You killed a boy," they shouted at him. "How could you kill Waddell? He never did you any harm."

"But I, but Major Pendleton said..." Larry stammered in his defense.

"Grab him, take him to the stockade. Gen. Hardee can sort this out. He deserves to be hung."

Lance watched as Hawk hurried away. Then he turned his attention to the boy at his feet. He leaned down, picked him up gently, and carried him back to the tent.

By the time Waddell was placed on his cot, he

was beginning to stir. "What happened?" he asked. "Where's Buttercup? Did you see Pendleton's face, Lance? Boy was he mad."

Lance stared at him in disbelief. "You're alive? How could you be alive? Do you know how much trouble you've caused?"

"Course I'm alive. Why wouldn't I be?"

"Larry shot you. In the back. Hawk said you were dead. I'm supposed to be burying…"

Lance ran out of the tent and to the road, shouting for Hawk. His friend was gone. The crowd had dispersed, the excitement over.

Hawk rode to Mariah at breakneck speed. The streets were crowded with fleeing civilians. Freed slaves wandered around, seemingly lost as to what to do next. He saw smoke in the distance, at the government complex. That was probably the Confederate governor, burning his own records.

But he saw no Yankees burning the city and raping the women.

By the time he got to Sally's, he realized the truth.

Rumors. He'd let rumors guide his better judgment. Rumors, the shooting of Waddell, and his own disgust with the war had caused him to act irrationally.

He'd deserted. He hated deserters. Now he was one of them.

He mounted the steps to Sally's house. The women were in the parlor discussing what McAllister had told them.

"Is it true, Hawk?" Mariah ran to him in a panic. "Waddell is dead? We have Buttercup in the barn. McAlli...er...Capt. Murray told us that Waddell had been shot. He had to leave before he gave us the details."

"It's true. I think it's true. I should have examined him more carefully but he seemed to be dead. I had to get to you. We heard rumors of rapes and murders."

"It's been quiet around here. Some people are leaving, but there's no need." Then Mariah realized the ramifications of Hawk's presence with them. "You just left?" she asked. "Did you have permission?"

"No. I deserted. I've got to go back and face my punishment."

"Punishment? But the war's over. Surely you won't be punished."

"It's possible. We're still at war and Gov. Vance ordered all deserters executed."

"Hawk, no! No!"

"It's unlikely. Gen. Hardee is a reasonable man. He knows I've been a good soldier. I'll have to beg for his mercy.

"Give me some lemonade. Better yet, give me something stronger. I need to plan what I'll say to the General."

Chapter 19

Hawk stayed with Mariah for the night. "Even though things are quiet, I want to be sure it stays that way," he reasoned. Spending the night in his wife's arms was an added incentive.

Try as he might, he could think of no better defense than his honor as a soldier. Hardee would have to decide what to do.

Hawk was up and dressed before sunrise. "I have to go," he whispered, leaning over the bed and kissing his wife for the last time. "The sooner I get this over with the better."

"Will you be all right?"

"Whatever happens, Mariah, know that I love you. If I don't live another day, the time I've spent with you will be the highlight of my life."

As he walked to the stable for his horse, Mariah came running after him. "Here, sign these," she said, thrusting the marriage certificate into Hawk's hands. Sally and Mary have witnessed it. Maybe if you sign it we can make it official, even without Waddell's signature."

Hawk took the papers and smiled. Leaning against a fence post, he signed his name with relish. "Now you're an honorable woman, Mrs. Hawkins. You don't have to worry about that anymore."

He kissed her again and then went into the barn to saddle his horse and ride to face the outcome of his actions.

It was still dark when Hawk got back to camp. He hoped no one saw him as he slipped into the compound and made his way to his tent. Waddell and Lance were inside, snoring softly.

"Waddell, you're alive," Hawk shouted in spite of himself.

The startled boy rolled over on his cot and fell out of bed. "'Course I'se alive, and now I'se got bruises to prove it."

"But I pronounced you dead. My corpses don't come back to life."

By now, Lance was awake and sitting up, rubbing sleep out of his eyes. "He must have had the wind knocked out of him when he fell off Buttercup. In your hurry to get to Mariah, you didn't wait to find out. I guess she's safe, otherwise you wouldn't have come back. But you should have stayed away.

"Couldn't do that," Hawk sat down on a campstool and rubbed the back of his neck. "I had to come back and beg Gen. Hardee for mercy."

"That may not be so easy. Hardee's not here—he had to go to the Capitol for the surrender. He'll be gone at least two days. Pendleton's in charge."

"Pendleton? That fool?"

"He is the ranking officer. Hardee had no choice. I understand he told Pendleton to keep things calm and not do anything stupid."

"Then I'll stay in the tent until Hardee gets back. I don't think anyone noticed when I came in."

But he was wrong. Around eight o'clock four soldiers came to his tent to arrest him. "Capt. Hawkins," the sergeant in charge read from a paper, "you are charged with desertion and dereliction of duty. Yesterday, at two o'clock in the afternoon, you left your assigned post and were not seen until five o'clock this morning. You are to accompany us to the brig."

"Barney," Lance grabbed the sergeant's arm. "What are you doing? This is Hawk. He sewed up your good for nothing hide when you got shot."

The sergeant looked at his feet. "I have my orders," he mumbled.

The trial was a joke. Larry, Pendleton's lackey, argued the case against Hawk. "I saw him," he chortled. "I saw him with my own eyes. He went flying out of here yesterday afternoon without anyone's permission. He went to see some woman, I'm told. Probably some hussy."

"Why you..." Lance and Barnes grabbed Hawk's arms to keep him from attacking the man. "That woman is my wife. I was concerned for her safety. And why aren't you in jail? You shot Waddell in the back."

Pendleton wrapped on the table. "Larry was released because he didn't do anything. Waddell wasn't hit by a bullet. He was up and walking around shortly after the incident.

"You are a different matter, Capt. Hawkins. Did you leave your duty post at approximately two o'clock yesterday afternoon?"

"Well yes, but...,"Hawk struggled to regain his composure. Again he stumbled toward his accusers and was held back by his friends.

"Don't cause anymore trouble, Hawk," Lance advised. "Pendleton is just looking for an excuse to ruin you."

Pendleton smirked. "And you did not return until the early hours this morning."

"That's right, but...," Hawk stood still, but his face contorted in fury.

"Then by the authority given me by Gen. William J. Hardee and under the direction of North Carolina Gov. Vance, I declare that you are a deserter and sentence you to hang by the neck until you are dead."

Hawk and Lance exchanged shocked glances, and then Lance began to laugh. "Pendleton, you're hilarious. I thought I just heard you say you were going to hang Hawk. Even you couldn't be that stupid."

"Oh, believe me. I'm quite serious. I'm in charge of this camp and Hawk will hang. He will be accompanied to his death by Pvt. Billy Potter, another deserter. He will be dead by noon."

"Noon!" Lance shouted. "You can't do that, Pendleton. Gen. Hardee will be furious. At least wait until he comes back."

"Noon. The sooner this sorry business is over, the better."

Sergeant Barney and his men came to escort Hawk back to his cell. Pendleton pushed Hawk's chest with his index finger, then turned on his heel and marched off with assumed self importance.

"Don't worry, Hawk," Lance shouted as his friend was led away. "I'll ride to town and find Hardee. I'll ride like the wind."

Gen. Hardee scowled at the soldier who interrupted his meeting. "Can't I even leave my command long enough to surrender with dignity?" he growled at the cowering man.

"S-sir," the messenger stammered. "It involves Hawk, your surgeon. I understand it's an emergency."

Hardee met Lance in the hallway. One look at the man's face told him that the situation was dire. As Lance blurted out the circumstances, Hardee became furious.

"Pendleton did what?" Hardee's voice rose to a crescendo and his face turned bright red. "That idiot!

That pompous, stupid idiot. I told him to keep the peace, not create havoc."

The last was said as he ran down the Capitol steps and called for his horse.

Forty-five minutes later, two soldiers Hawk had never seen before came for him. They bound his hands and manhandled him from his cell. Pendleton met them, his face glowing with importance.

"It's not noon," Hawk shouted. "You said noon."

"I said you'd be dead by noon. You deserve to die. You think you're better than everyone else, toting that little black boy everywhere you go. Our Confederate boys have died in vain if you become a father to that kid."

"Lead him out boys," Pendleton told the guards. "Lead him out and let's be done with it."

Hawk smiled a faint smile and began a slow, measured step over the 100 yards from the holding cell to the gallows. He mounted the stairs with the same dignity he'd shown all his life.

Hawk did not know the priest who held a small cross and stood by the two nooses. The man mumbled something Hawk chose to ignore—something about forgive them their sins.

On the top step, Hawk stumbled and was caught by a guard. "Scared?" the soldier asked. "You should be, Johnny Reb."

Hawk looked over the crowd. There were

Northern sympathizers, soldiers in blue uniforms, released slaves, women wearing blue ribbons in their hair or pinned to their dress. Raleigh had always been a divided city. Today, the Confederates were in hiding. This group wanted Southern blood. Executed by one of their own? Even better.

Gen. Hardee and Lance rode hard, but precious time had elapsed. As they neared the camp, they saw the gallows in the distance. Built as a necessity, but never used, the scaffold had been convenient for Pendleton's cruelty.

Firing their pistols and whipping their horses until their hides oozed sweat, the desperate soldier's cries went unheard at the execution. Barely visible on the horizon, Hardee and Lance saw two men being led up the steps of the gallows. They watched in horror as the two were pushed across the platform and each positioned under a noose. "Stop! Stop!" they continued to shout at the top of their lungs, but the distance was too great.

Hawk struggled, trying to pull away from his captors, but Pendleton had chosen the strongest guards he could find.

Surely Lance would return in time or Pendleton would come to his senses, content to have scared everyone. But no, a burlap bag was fitted over his face and the rope lowered around his neck.

In the distance he heard Waddell wailing. Then the boy cried out, "I loves you Hawk. You'se my people. I'll take care of Mariah."

Hawk thought he heard gunshots and distant cries of "Stop! Halt!" But Pendleton didn't stop. "Do it! Now!" Pendleton shouted. "Now, I say!"

Hawk felt a heavy weight at his neck and the light seeping through the burlap turned black. The crowd heard a sharp twang as the ropes pulled tight, breaking the necks of the two prisoners.

Somewhere, high in a lone pine tree, a red-tailed hawk screeched an ominous death knell and the witnesses shivered with terror.

"You idiot!" Hardee screamed as he faced Pendleton. "I told you not to cause trouble. Instead you created it."

"I was doing my duty, General. You left me in charge." Pendleton puffed out his chest with self-importance, but his eyes would not meet those of his commanding officer. "These men deserted. Punishment was quick and sure."

"I'll have you court-martialed if it's the last thing I do. The war is almost over. We just surrendered Raleigh."

Chapter 20

Mariah watched through the long windows of Sally's parlor as three men and a boy rode to the front gate. "Why there's Lance and Barnes," she told Sally. "And Waddell is with them. I don't know the other man, but it must be Gen. Hardee. I wonder where Hawk is."

Sally turned and shot a knowing look to Mary but said nothing. Slow realization of the truth clouded Mariah's mind. In an effort to forestall the inevitable, she focused on the mundane.

"Why is Waddell riding behind Lance?" she asked. "Oh, I remember, we have Buttercup in our barn." Then she fainted.

When she came to, she was lying on a couch in the parlor. Gen. Hardee came and took her hand.

"I'm so sorry, Mrs. Hawkins. This war has been hard on all of us—but especially the innocent. Hawk was one of the finest men I ever knew."

The men didn't stay long. "I do need to ask you something, Mrs. Hawkins." The General had saved this unpleasant task until the end. "What should we do with the body? Where do you want Hawk buried?"

"Here. We'll bury him here with my father and the rest of my people. I must contact his sisters. They don't even know that Hawk and I are married."

"Come on, then," the General said. "We need to get back to camp. Go get Buttercup, Waddell."

"I ain't going with you, General. I promised Hawk I'd take care of Mariah. They'se my people now."

The war ended. Gen. Lee surrendered the Army of Northern Virginia at Appomattox. The Confederates tried to rebuild their lives.

"Waddell and I must get back to Lockwood Folly," Mariah told Sally one bright morning in mid May. I can resume teaching in the fall and we can try to farm our home place."

Sally was preoccupied, as she'd been for the past week. Mariah couldn't leave her in this state.

"What's bothering you, Sally?" she asked. "We can't go home with you acting like this. You couldn't take care of yourself."

Sally looked at Mariah and began to cry. "It's Capt. Murray," she whispered. "The war is over—has been for weeks—and he hasn't come to me. We said such sweet things to each other. I can't believe he was leading me on."

Mariah looked at the sobbing girl in amazement. She really didn't know the truth. It was time she learned.

"I have to tell you about Murray, Sally. That wasn't his name at all. It was McAllister. Capt. Jacob McAllister of the Union Army—a spy and a master of disguise."

"I don't believe you. How would you know anyway?"

"Because he passed his secrets to me. I brought him gold and he gave me information. I turned this over to our Confederate forces. Some of what he told me was quite useful."

"I don't believe you! Murray is a loyal Confederate. And even if what you say is true, I don't care. Murray, McAllister, whatever. I love him and I'm worried about him."

"Well, there are still lots of Yankees in Raleigh. In fact, there's a large encampment outside of town. But we can't just go waltzing in there and ask for him. They wouldn't give information to local women."

"I can." Waddell had come in from the kitchen and overheard the last of the conversation. "A little black boy could slip in real easy. They'd think I was a freed slave and probably invite me to dinner."

"It might work," Mariah agreed. "McAllister knows you, but the others don't."

"Pull-eeze let me go. I'se gots to get away from Mary. She's either got me doing my lessons or working in the kitchen. I ain't no kitchen boy."

"Then go," Sally insisted. "Go now. Mariah and I will drive you in the buggy and you can walk the rest of the way. We'll come back for you tomorrow."

Waddell located McAllister with little trouble. "Jacob McAllister?" a Yankee soldier laughed when the boy approached him. "How do you know that rascal? He's in the brig—charged with spying. Soon as some sort of evidence is found, he'll be swinging from a rope."

Charmer that he was, Waddell soon convinced the guards to let him speak to McAllister.

"Yassir, I knows Capt. McAllister. He hepped my mammy during the war. She'll tan my hide if'n I don't find out what's going on."

"Waddell!" McAllister was overjoyed to see him. "How's Mariah? How's Sally? I'll go see them as soon as I get out of here."

"Miss Mariah get herself married to Lt. Hawk. Fact is, I performed the ceremony." The boy's chest swelled with pride, then deflated. "But Hawk is dead and Miss Sally is a'pining for you. Can't figure out why you ain't been by to see her."

"I've been stuck in here, that's why. They're looking everywhere for evidence I was a spy. They've found some Confederate from Willard, North Carolina who said I killed his buddy after I got information from them. "

"Miss Sally shore has been been worried 'bout you. Can I stay with you tonight.? They's gonna pick me up tomorrow but I ain't got nowhere to sleep til then."

"It's a little unusual," the guard said when asked. "But I guess it'll be all right. Just be gone first thing in the morning."

"Send Sally my love," McAllister told the boy as he was leaving. "And if she can help me, I sure would be grateful."

Waddell was right. Sally was ecstatic when told that McAllister was still in Raleigh and sent his regards. "Oh, Mariah!" she exclaimed. "We've got to help him. One hanging is enough."

Poor Sally wasn't an astute creature. She chatted away, oblivious to the sad pall that had settled over Mariah and Waddell.

When they got back to Sally's home, Mariah went to her bedroom. Opening a bureau drawer, she removed a soft cloth and held it in trembling hands—the Medal of Honor that Betsy had stolen from McAllister's saddlebags.

"This would prove his guilt," she whispered. "If I showed this to the Yankees and told my story, McAllister would hang. On the other hand, this medal might prove useful in another way."

She didn't consider long. McAllister had rescued Buttercup. And Sally had been good to her and Waddell. She was tired of war and death. Sally deserved some happiness and she would help if she could.

She wrapped the medal back up and called for

Waddell. "We have to go back to the prison," she told him. "I have to see McAllister myself."

The next morning she and Waddell drove back to the camp. She'd told Sally she had errands. The fewer people who knew about this, the better.

"This is my mistress," Waddell told the guard. "She needs to see Capt. McAllister about some unfinished business."

"And what business might that be?" the guard asked, grinning at Mariah with obvious interest.

"McAllister has something that belonged to my family and I want it back." She smiled shyly at the guard from under her straw hat.

"Well, it can't matter. If you can get anything from that old fox, good for you. He'll hang soon enough anyway."

"Mariah!" McAllister was thrilled to see her. "Did you bring my deliverance?"

"Perhaps. That depends on you." She opened the cloth and showed him the medal—careful to hold it out of his reach.

"What's this? Well I'll be. My Medal of Honor. How in the world did you get this? Give it to me. They wouldn't dare execute a Medal of Honor winner, even if the devil himself testified against me.

"I'll give it to you—for a price. Marry Sally. Be good to her. She deserves nothing else. Reform your ways and become a good citizen."

"Oh I will, I will. I'll be the model of a good husband, find a job, and live a quiet, respectable life."

Mariah held the medal out to the excited man. "If you go back on your word, McAllister, I'll see that you regret it. I'll hound you the rest of your life and make you pay for your sins."

Chapter 21

McAllister was released. His first stop was at the home on Oak Street. "How did you get the medal, Mariah?" he asked when they were alone. "I have a right to know."

"No you don't. It was taken to be used against you. Be thankful that you've done enough good things in your life that I decided otherwise."

He and Sally soon left for Barbados. Sally was beside herself with joy. "Oh, Mariah! I'll miss you. What will you do?"

"I'm still going back to Lockwood Folly. I'm taking Waddell and Mary with me."

"No!" Waddell shouted from the other room. "Not Mary. She'll be a'nagging me all the time. I'se tired of that woman ordering me around."

"She wants you to learn, Waddell. If you're going to be a preacher, you've got to be able to read the Bible— even the hard parts. Besides, Mary has nowhere to go and we will need the help."

"We don't need no help, not from the likes of Mary. I can do the work, with just a little help from you."

"But can you take care of a baby? I need Mary to help me take care of the baby."

Waddell jutted out his chin, then the belligerent stare gave way to astonishment. "Baby?" he whispered. "Hawk's baby?

Mariah's Story is not Over....

The South is in ruins, yet life must go on. Mariah has responsibilities to herself, Hawk's baby, Waddell, Mary, Sally, and the children in eastern North Carolina—both black and white—who need an education.

Andrew Johnson is President of the restored nation after the death of Abraham Lincoln. He calls on Mariah for help with Reconstruction. Is she woman enough for the task?

Waddell is becoming a teenager. Can he reconcile his past and make a future for himself?

Will Sally's marriage last? Will McAllister make good his promise to be a faithful husband and upstanding citizen?

Will the red-tailed hawk continue to protect and guide Mariah and those she loves?

About the Author

Edith Edwards worked in the public schools as a speech therapist, teacher, and administrator for twenty-nine years. Now she lives and writes on the banks of the beautiful Lockwood Folly River with the love of her life, Don, and their Chiweenie, Rosie. They have two grown daughters and four amazing grandchildren. Helena Grace Upshaw, Edith's oldest granddaughter, is the model for this book cover.

Edith loves to hear from her readers. Contact her at *eaedwards@atmc.net* or visit her website *www.edithedwards.com.*

CPSIA information can be obtained at www.ICGtesting.com
Printed in the USA
BVOW04s0006241013

334505BV00008B/57/P